The Twin in the Tavern

Books by Barbara Brooks Wallace

Peppermints in the Parlor

The Barrel in the Basement

Perfect Acres, Inc.

The Twin in the Tavern

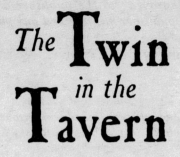

The Twin in the Tavern

Barbara Brooks Wallace

Aladdin Paperbacks

First Aladdin Paperbacks edition October 1995
Copyright © 1993 by Barbara Brooks Wallace

Aladdin Paperbacks
An imprint of Simon & Schuster
Children's Publishing Division
1230 Avenue of the Americas
New York, NY 10020

The Library of Congress has cataloged the hardcover edition
as follows:
Wallace, Barbara Brooks, date.
The twin in the tavern / Barbara Brooks Wallace.—1st ed.
p. cm.
"A Jean Karl book."
Summary: A young orphan, afraid of being sent to the
workhouse, finds himself at the mercy of the unsavory owner
of a tavern in Alexandria, Virginia, while he tries to solve
the mystery surrounding his past and a missing twin.
ISBN 0–689–31846–4
[1. Orphans—Fiction. 2. Twins—Fiction. 3. Mystery and
detective stories. 4. [Fic]] I. Title.
PZ7.W1547Tw 1993 92-36429
ISBN 0–689–80167–X (Aladdin pbk.)

For my very own granddaughter, Victoria,
Her very own book, with love

Table of Contents

The Twin in the Tavern

Chapter I
Toady

Wind, sharp and cruel, howled down the road and attacked the small cottage, rattling shutters and hurling sheets of freezing rain and sleet against the windows. Alone inside, Taddy crouched behind the old pine rocking chair in a corner of the front room, cramped and chilled from having hidden there the better part of the day. He curled his arms around his knees and tried to huddle more deeply into the worn gray blanket wrapped around his shoulders.

Eeeee! Eeeee! The hinges on the shutters squealed in agony as the wind tried to rip them away. A terrible final squeal followed by a bang! bang! thump! announced that one shutter, at least, had finally parted company from the cottage. Taddy dug deeper into the corner.

If only Mr. and Mrs. Thomas, the neighbors who lived but a mile away, would come! But when Taddy had arrived on their doorstep to tell them his Uncle and Aunt Buntz were no more, taken in two short days by the dread disease brought into the nearby seaport of Alexandria by the ship *Golden Gull,* the Thomases had fearfully drawn their children away from him. They told him to run back home at once and wait, and be a brave little lad. They would see to it, they said, that someone would come. And someone *had* come that very day. But it was two strange men with their frightening wagon, and Taddy hid from them in a cupboard the whole time they were there. Mr. and Mrs. Thomas never did appear, and Taddy knew now that they never would.

The only thing left for him to do was to run away. For what if there should be a second terrible knocking at the door, this time courtesy of strangers coming for *him*? Twice orphaned now, though he was not yet turned eleven, Taddy knew of the fate of those who were so much as once orphaned—the dreaded workhouse! Lucky to escape it the first time, how could he expect to be so lucky the second? Perhaps he ought to leave at once and not wait for the murderous storm to end. After all, though the night was half over, someone could still come for him at any moment.

Almost as if it were taunting him, the wind screamed around the cottage and forced its way through cracks in the door. His uncle's rocking chair, caught in the draft, began to rock slowly back and forth. Creak! Creak! Back and forth with no one in it. Taddy's attempts at being "a brave little lad" finally crumpled. He threw his head onto his arms and sobbed.

Bang! Bang! Bang! Another shutter clattered as it took leave of the cottage. A few moments passed and bang! bang! bang! again. Yet another was gone. Or was it? Was not that banging and rattling coming from the direction of the front door? The banging continued, leaving no doubt at last as to what it meant. Someone was at the front door! Taddy swiftly pulled the blanket over his head, allowing only the barest sliver of an opening for one wide, frightened eye to peer through.

Bang! Bang! Bang! The door crashed against the wall as it flew open. Heavy footsteps caused the pine floor of the cottage to tremble as they stomped into the room, accompanied by the sounds of someone grunting and breathing heavily. But the slamming shut of that same door was followed by a sudden, wary silence. Then there was the sound of a match striking, and a lantern flared up.

Through the spindles of the rocking chair, Taddy could make out a dark shape—no, *shapes,* for there were two of them, two men in caped slickers, shiny and black as wet coal. Excepting that one man came only to the shoulders of the other, who held the lantern, little could be told about them. For their faces were hidden in shadows under the brims of their black sou'wester oiled hats. But they had gone absolutely still again, like huge birds of prey standing with their heads cocked—listening.

Finally, the shorter of the two men spoke in a gravelly whisper. "Don't hear nothing, Neezer. Do you?"

"Not when you're bellowing in my ear, Lucky, you and that miserable wind," growled the man addressed as Neezer. "Put a stopper in it, will you?"

He strode quickly but cautiously to the back of the cottage and waved the lantern inside each of the two small rooms he found there. "Nobody!" he announced gruffly.

Lucky shuddered and looked nervously over his shoulder at the front door. "Why don't that wind stop permanent?"

"You best say thanks for that wind," Neezer replied.

"We both know 'twas the only reason 'twas safe for us to come and cart this stuff away. No one else got the courage."

"For more reasons'n just one," Lucky grumbled.

Neezer turned on him with a snarl. "Now don't you go starting that again. Come on, let's get this stuff out before we get caught and get ourselves interduced to the jailhouse." He lifted one end of the kitchen table, which was also the dining table. "I need a hand. You just going to stand there?"

Lucky shuffled his feet around but stayed rooted to the spot. "You certain everyone's gone?"

"*Both* dead and gone, courtesy of them cheerful grave merchants, Murdstone and Murdstone, Inc. I told you I heard it myself from their miserable blue lips, though they was too scairt to come themselves and sent some poor idiots to do the job. But you already been told that," Neezer snapped. "And if you desire to share in the profits of this business venture, you best get yourself over here."

This last statement was clearly what was needed to inspire Lucky to action. Within moments, he and Neezer were lugging the furnishings of the cottage through the front door.

In the meantime, Taddy's feelings, hidden by the blanket along with their owner, went from terror to blazing anger. Thieves! That is what these two were—thieves! And they were stealing his dear aunt and uncle's furnishings. He watched in helpless rage and despair at the disappearance of the set of blue flowered china, chipped and cracked it was true, but still treasured by his Aunt Buntz. Then there went the familiar little rough-hewn dining chairs made by his Uncle Buntz. One pitiful possession followed another, accompanied by the complaints of Lucky.

"The horse and the cow and chickens I could see the worth of. But all this junk don't seem worth the risk."

"Hmmmph!" snorted Neezer. "If you can figger a way to drag a horse, a cow, and a pack of squawking chickens along in the middle of night with no notice being taken of 'em, and then figger where we can hide 'em, I'll take my hat off to you. Anyway, anything what brings in money's worth the risk, if arrangements ain't impossible. That's my motto, and been it long as I can remember. How do you think I come by being owner of the Dog's Tail? Risks for money, that's how, no matter what the measly amount."

This impressive bit of economic wisdom silenced Lucky for a few moments as he stumped over and picked up the rocking chair behind which Taddy was crouching. And Taddy's blazing anger turned suddenly back to heart-stopping, freezing terror. In his fury over what was happening to his aunt and uncle's treasured belongings, he had forgotten that his hiding place might be suddenly snatched away.

But it appeared that Neezer's "motto" had not simmered and brewed in Lucky's brain long enough to make a dent, for he paid no attention to the heaped-up blanket behind the rocker. It did not, however, escape Neezer's sharp eyes, and Taddy's trembling hope that he might be spared lasted but one short moment.

"Don't go leaving that stuff in the corner!" Neezer barked. "Take it with the chair!"

"Aw, Neezer, it's just rags," whined Lucky.

"Didn't you hear one miserable thing what I told you? Rags may be rags, but there's no such thing in this world named as *just* rags. There's somebody someplace wants rags, and willing to pay for 'em. You mark my words."

With a sullen look on his face, Lucky balanced the rocking chair on his hip and with his free hand snatched up the blanket. Then he stood there staring, his eyes popped and speech clearly knocked right out of him at the sight of the small, frozen statue that was Taddy.

"So, rags is it?" shouted Neezer triumphantly. "Never in my borned days seen rags with arms, legs, and a head on 'em. And you was just going to leave 'em there."

"W-wh-wh-what's *he* doing here?" stammered Lucky.

Suspicion darted from between Neezer's narrowed eyelids. "Murdstone and Murdstone reported as how there was a boy somewheres around, but when they sent for them other bodies, his weren't here. Where was you, boy? Speak up!" Neezer's eyelids flew open, allowing Taddy full benefit of a pair of glaring eyes as dark and mean and wickedly cruel as a pair could get that belong to a human being.

"I-I've been here all along . . . h-h-hiding," said Taddy, gulping.

"All along!" shrieked Lucky, letting the rocking chair drop with a clatter and hurling the blanket into a far corner of the room. "All along, Neezer! That means he could o' got it from them and passed it along of us. Oh, I should never o' come. All for a bunch o' junk and a pile o' rags! And what's the use o' selling *nothing* if you're stony cold in your grave and too dead to enjoy it?"

But the look of sudden shock that had leaped into Neezer's face at this thought was gone in an instant. "Don't be a dolt, Lucky. If he was going to get it, he'd of got it by now and been six feet under . . ." Neezer paused to reconsider that statement, ". . . or ready for that particular location, anyways."

"You . . . you certain?" asked Lucky.

"Certain enough. But also certain, and what's more important, he's seen more than he ought." Neezer's eyes narrowed again to the same suspicious slivers. "What kind of plans you got for what you seen here tonight, boy? And don't look so stupid at me. I'm asking if you had plans to run blabbing to friends, or maybe relations."

"I . . . I have none!" Taddy blurted. And he realized at once from the sudden, barely suppressed grin on Neezer's face that he had made a grim mistake.

"So," said Neezer, "it looks as if you've gone and got yourself orphaned. And there's none the wiser if you just happens to do a vanishing act, eh?"

With this, Lucky, who had been staring with slack-jawed wonder at this new development, suddenly tugged anxiously at Neezer's coat sleeve. "What's that mean, Neezer? What you got in mind?"

Neezer's eyebrows raised. "Why, if something happens to the boy, like maybe a fatal accident, who's to know . . . or care?"

Lucky backed away from him as if he were a burning coal. "No! No! Not me you don't get into something like that, Neezer. Worst you can get from stealing's the jail-house. I ain't taking my chances on the hangman's noose."

"You got a better idea?" Neezer growled.

Lucky scratched his head for a moment, then rubbed his nose for another, and finally pulled Neezer aside for a whispered conference. That ended to Neezer's apparent satisfaction, his attention snapped back to Taddy. His face took on a sly, questioning look.

"You know about the workhouse, boy?"

Oh yes, Taddy knew all about *that*! For had he not been reminded again and again of how glad Aunt and Uncle Buntz were that they had saved him from the workhouse, by bringing him from New York when his mama and papa had met their fate in a terrible train accident? The workhouse was "a fate as grim as death," Aunt Buntz always said. Oh yes, Taddy did indeed know about the workhouse!

Slowly, he nodded.

"Well, I can see from the look on your face you'll be mighty pleased to know that we got another plan for you. Plan two, you might say." Oozing an oily, confidential air, Neezer shoved his face up close to Taddy. "Now, how'd you like to come live someplace where you get a nice warm place to sleep, good meals served regular, and no questions asked? None at all! You'd like that, wouldn't you?"

Taddy nodded again, not quite so slowly.

"Of course," Neezer went on, "bed and meals don't come free. You'll have to do a chore or two around the Dog's Tail, which you doubtless recognizes as a famous hostelry in Alexandria. But you got to admit that sounds better than any trip to the workhouse, eh?"

Taddy hardly dared mention that this was the first time he had ever heard of the Dog's Tail, much less recognize it as a famous hostelry. But it was certain that anything sounded better than the workhouse. He hardly needed a moment's thought before giving another nod.

All at once, however, the oily air vanished, and

Neezer's face swiftly turned hard and ugly again. "But mind you," he snarled, "you blab about what you seen here tonight, and the bargain's off. Further, you try running away, and you'll find we got more arms and longer ones than you ever heard of to snatch you back. You got that clear?"

This time Taddy's nod was twice as quick as all the rest.

"Hmmmph!" Neezer grunted, turning to Lucky. "This being your idea, it better be a good one. He's a skinny little runt, and doubtless this plan of yours does more good for him than it ever might for the Dog's Tail. We'll see."

"Why not let him start now?" Lucky said. "Help us get this stuff out."

Neezer shrugged. "What's your name, boy?"

"T-T-Taddy."

"What kind of name's that?" growled Neezer. "Don't like it."

Lucky sniggered. "Whyn't you call him . . . Toady? The Dog's Tail got something what skitters, so now you can have one what hops. Hop, hop, hop, Neezer!"

"Toady? Sounds good to me." Neezer looked Taddy up and down, and suddenly his whiskered face was split in two by a broad grin.

It was a chilling grin, one that seemed to give promise of more terrors, some perhaps more frightening than those that had most recently taken place. What was meant by it? And what kind of bargain was it that Taddy had just made with these two?

Chapter II
A Fearsome Journey

Shoved into the back of the wagon with less care than if he had been an old, shabby chair or table, Taddy lay curled around his small bundle of clothes tied in a kitchen rag, a shivering, miserable ball under the clammy oilskin cover. The uneven wagon wheels squealed and groaned under him, pitching him back and forth almost as if they were trying to hurl him from the wagon.

Clop! Clop! Clop!

The muffled beat of the horse's hooves was a dismal accompaniment to the words that drummed through Taddy's head.

Hop! Hop! Hop!

Something what skitters!

Something what hops!

A toad was what hopped, and now Toady was the name he would be called. Still, what difference did a name make now? He would answer to anything they chose if it meant food and a warm place to sleep—and no workhouse!

Clop! Clop! Clop!

Would this ride never end? Was the town of Alexandria so far away? Taddy had never thought so, but then he had never been there. Alexandria! The farmer's market was there, where Uncle Buntz went to sell milk and eggs, fruits and vegetables grown on their small farm, and the sparkling jams and jellies preserved by Aunt Buntz. Then home Uncle Buntz would return, bringing flour and salt, sugar and molasses, and sometimes a bolt of sturdy cotton fabric or a packet of pins for Aunt Buntz.

To Taddy, Alexandria sounded like a wonderfully exciting place. How many times had he pleaded to go along with his uncle, or with his uncle and aunt when he was old enough to be left safely alone at home? But he had never been allowed to go. Why?

One day, when he was lying on the floor by his cot, studying the reading lesson just given him by Aunt Buntz, he heard them talking. They must have thought he had gone out to play but even so talked in lowered voices that could barely be heard.

"He's gone and asked again to go to Alexandria," his uncle said. "Someday he's got to be told about the danger."

"Not now, please! Not yet!" his aunt had replied, a real note of fear in her voice. "He's still so young, he might just say something to someone without thinking. We long since agreed that when he was twelve was the time to tell him. Let's have no more said about it!"

Tell Taddy *what*? Have no more said about *what*? Oh, if only he had jumped up from the floor and asked them right then and there. But he knew this had been a conversation not meant for his ears. How could he confess that he had been lying there all along eavesdropping?

But now they were both gone, and there was no one left to tell him anything. What was the danger spoken of in such fearful tones? What was the mystery?

And then all at once, something seemed to explode inside Taddy's head. It was the words his uncle had barely managed to whisper hoarsely in the final moments of his life. In all the misery, fear, and horror of what was happening, those words had simply vanished from Taddy's mind. Now, suddenly, the words spoken with such effort came back to him.

"Nothing is what you think. You are not really ours, Taddy. Forgive us for not ever telling you. There was too much danger for you if we did. But . . . but find your twin, Taddy. Find your twin and you . . . you will know who you are. But be careful. Be careful, lad. Trust . . . no one!"

And then his uncle was gone, and those words with him. Until now.

Nothing is what you think. You are not really ours. Did that not mean his dear Aunt and Uncle Buntz had not really been his aunt and uncle? And what of his mama and papa? Had they really met their fate in a train wreck?

Nothing is what you think. Nothing! Did that also mean that he had not been born in and brought from New York while still a baby, as he had been told? Where from, then? Was it—was it Alexandria, where the danger was? Alexandria! Where he was now headed with two men who thought nothing of robbery, and one of whom who was not above doing worse than that. And Taddy Buntz's life was in their hands! No, not Taddy Buntz, for if he had never belonged to his aunt and uncle, that could not be his name anymore. He was now just Taddy Somebody. Or more likely, Toady Nobody!

But then what was that other thing his Uncle Buntz had said? *Find your twin and you will know who you are.* A twin! The rest was hard enough to believe, but this was so farfetched that it could only have been invented by a fevered brain. Yet, what if it were as true as the rest? Somehow, somewhere, there might be a boy Taddy's age who looked just like him! Where would the boy live? Would it not be Alexandria? Was he in danger too?

And what of those ominous warnings? *Be careful! Trust no one!* How was Taddy to discover anything if he was to trust no one, talk to no one?

Twin! Twin! Aunt and uncle not his aunt and uncle! Twin! Twin! *Nothing is what you think! Trust no one! Be careful!*

The words began to whirl around in his head. Around and around until he could no longer separate one word or thought from the other. If only there were someone who could help him make sense of it all. But there was no one now. He was all alone. Worse than that, an *orphan* all alone and in danger. From what? From whom? *Trust no one! Be careful!* Clop! Clop! Clop! The hoofbeats drummed endlessly on.

Then all at once the wagon, providing a bumpy enough ride as it was, began to buck up and down and rock in the most perilous manner. Terrified, Taddy clutched onto the nearest solid object he could find in darkness thick as pitch, hanging on for his life with hands grown numb with cold. The thumping and rocking continued, but he finally accepted that he was not near imminent death from being catapulted out of the wagon. Although still holding tightly with one hand, he managed with the other to lift a flap of the oilskin cover and peer out.

Although they could barely be seen under a gaslight fluttering weakly overhead, it was clear that what had been making the wagon dance about so savagely was nothing more than ordinary *cobblestones*! But Taddy had no more than made this discovery than it all struck him. Cobblestones and street gaslights! That could only mean they had arrived in the city at last! Yet what a different arrival it was from any he had ever imagined.

Instead of humming with the sounds of a busy city on market day, the street lay deserted between houses all pressed together like so many brick and wood boxes. And Taddy himself, instead of perched safely in the comforting protective care of Aunt and Uncle Buntz, was being flung about in the back of a wagon driven by a pair of thieves.

Clop! Clop! Clop! Thump! *Thump!* The wagon gave a last violent shudder as it left the cobblestoned street and lumbered around a corner. Now, on one side of the street they had entered were what appeared to be rows of tall, bony fingers reaching for the dark sky, with small lanterns dancing in the wind below them. These ghostly fingers were the ships' masts of the famed Alexandria waterfront!

Taddy had only just taken in this eerie scene, however, when his eyes were caught and held by a narrow building of some three stories looming in the shadows across from the dockside. The light from two gas lamps on either side of its large, forbidding door was all but swallowed up by brick walls as black as the inside of a chimney from age and neglect. Shutters that had clearly been paid no atten-

tion from the day they had been hung a
dangled crazily from every window.

This might have been any old waterfront
a dozen others, but for one important differen
up the wall beside the door, an arm of rough w
out. Shackled to it by a pair of rusty chains, there
sign. The flickering gaslights licked at a faded pain
a grinning white dog and tarnished gold letters that read
DOG'S TAIL. So this was the place Neezer had described as
a "famous hostelry"! But unless the inside of the building
told a far different story from the outside, these high-
sounding words must have been something he invented
himself. Taddy rubbed his eyes and looked harder at the
dingy sign. Any question he might have had, however, as
to what this building could be was immediately put to
rest when the wagon turned into the alley that ran next to
it, then turned again and came to a grinding, groaning
stop. He had thought his heart had sunk as low as it
could ever sink, only to discover that it could sink a great
deal lower. For there was nothing left now to dispel the
grim fact that this dark, deadly building, guarded by a
dog with a murderously evil grin on his face, was about to
become Taddy's new home.

Chapter III
The Dog's Tail

A thump! followed by a second thump! told Taddy that the men had jumped from the wagon. Two sets of footsteps crunched heavily on coarse gravel as they stumped around to the rear. Then the oilskin was roughly untied and jerked off. Waving an oil lantern over Taddy's head, Neezer examined the contents of the wagon. The smoky light of the lantern picked up the suspicious glints in his narrowed eyes.

"Hmmmph!" he snorted. "Appears to be nothing missing. You see anything missing, Lucky?"

Lucky's eyes slowly inspected the contents of the wagon. Then he rubbed his chin and slowly inspected again. But though Taddy appeared to be paid no more attention than a shadow cast by the lantern, it was clear that this performance was directed at him. Did they really think that a small, skinny boy, blue with cold and fright, could untie and remove the oilskin cover (allowing that he wanted to do it!), lift a piece of furniture from the moving wagon, and make off with it into the stormy night? Or even if he could have managed to commit the crime, that he actually would return and remain under their very noses? He stared up at them with the fixed eyes of a rabbit trapped by a pair of foxes.

Lucky enjoyed yet another round of chin rubbing and inspection before he delivered his verdict. "Not certain, Neezer. But I guess it 'pears to me likewise as how nothing's missing. Good luck for *someone*."

"Rare good luck," agreed Neezer. He unlatched the tailgate of the wagon. "So let's get started."

"Aw, whyn't we just leave it for the night," Lucky whined. "We go lugging this stuff out now, might be we'll wake up all the lodgers."

"Don't be a dolt!" said Neezer. "When did we ever leave stuff sitting outside in the wagon? It goes back to the storage shed right now like all the other times. There it stays all cozy and locked up a day or so until arrangements is made to get rid of it. You need to get your head looked inside of if you think anything else, Lucky."

Lucky just threw out his hands to this. "Well, Toady gets to help, I presumes?"

Neezer nodded. "You presumes right. Why else was he brung? Now, just get him out of there."

Snap! Thick fingers locked around Taddy's wrists, yanked him from the wagon, and dropped him to the ground with no more care than if he had been a sack of dog scraps. A wooden chair was shoved roughly into his arms.

"Mind you don't drop it! Now, let's see you hop, hop, hop, Toady!"

"What he means is *march*!" snapped Neezer.

Stagger, however, was all Taddy could manage as he followed Neezer and Lucky around a small building that seemed to be crouching there just to make the journey to the shed more treacherous. Back and forth stumped the cheerless procession, enlivened only by Lucky giving Taddy a shove whenever the opportunity presented itself. Soon he felt every bone that he owned aching to the point that there was as much danger of *himself* dropping as anything he might be carrying.

But it was not until every last scrap of rag had been emptied from the wagon that Neezer finally bolted the shed door, locking it with not one but two well-rusted giant padlocks. Then he and Lucky trudged silently to the back door of the inn without so much as a nod in Taddy's direction. He could only suppose that he was meant to follow, so he snatched up his ragged bundle and stumbled after them.

The door they entered at the rear of the inn brought them into a room as dark as the moonless night outside. But the light from Neezer's lantern swinging from his hand was enough, even though barely, to show a not-too-large room made to appear even smaller by the great iron pots, pans, and other instruments of cooking dangling in higgledy-piggledy disarray from the ceiling, an enormous black iron stove hovering against a wall, and a worn pine worktable occupying most all the available space in the center. But even if this had not been pointed out by the moving lantern, the smell of old grease soaked into the woodwork from the bubblings, boilings, and burnings of several thousand dinners was enough to let Taddy know they were parading through a kitchen.

But the kitchen was not where this parade was to end, for the two men, with Taddy straggling along at their heels, strode quickly across it. Then, as Neezer snuffed out the light from his lantern, they pushed open a door into a dank room with a single gas lamp flickering thinly on a far wall. Eight or ten nondescript tables with mismatched chairs filled the space intended for half as many. The rest of the room held another painting of the same murderous dog that hung outside, several tarnished coat hooks on either side of the front door, a small counter, and a narrow staircase that rose steeply up one wall. Tiny pinpoints of light from the gas lamp marked rows of dusty bottles on shelves behind the counter. But although a heavy, stale reminder of food, drink, wet cloaks and boots hung in the air, the coat hooks and chairs were empty, and the room deserted.

There was scarcely time to note all this, however, when Neezer suddenly muttered a sharp oath, grabbed Lucky's arm to hold him back, and at the same time made a well-placed kick backward with his heavy boot at Taddy for the same purpose. A squeak of surprise and pain from Taddy was unfortunately rewarded with yet another kick.

"Who's there?" Neezer growled, addressing the far corner of the room. "Speak up, or you'll get something you never bargained for!"

It was then Taddy realized that the boot applied to his shins had nothing to do with something he had done wrong. For in the corner of the room, so deep in shadows it was easy to have missed him at first glance, a man sat.

"Now, now, gentlemen," he said in a voice that had the curious whispering sound of something gliding through tall grass. "No need to be disturbed. I was down here reading my book and clearly lost track of time. I had only just turned down my lamp." As if it needed proving, the man, with a deft twist of two fleshless pale fingers, turned up the lamp wick and held up a small black book over the lamp chimney for display. The lamp also cast its yellow gleam upon the man himself, revealing a long narrow face, with nose to match, and thin, moist lips drawn back to form a slippery smile over teeth that somehow, in size and color, resembled old piano keys.

In an instant, Neezer, who had so far done little else but snarl, snap, and growl to the degree that it might well have been his portrait hanging in the inn rather than that of the vicious dog, managed the most astonished turnabout in character.

"Oh, it's you, is it, Perfessor Greevey!" he said in a voice very different from the one with which Taddy had become familiar. Oil in the form of melted butter oozed from every syllable. "Sorry if we scairt you. No cause to leave on our account."

Before the man addressed as Professor Greevey had the chance to reply, however, a small face screwed up with fright under an oversized nightcap suddenly appeared at the top of the stairs, peering anxiously over the railing. "Oh! Oh! Oh! What is it? What is wrong?"

"Oh, go back to . . ." Neezer barked, and then remembering that present company was still present—and listening—caught himself and started again in a very different manner. "Nothing is wrong. Now you just go back to bed, dear Mrs. Scrat."

The frightened face disappeared as suddenly as it had appeared.

"Anything I can fetch you, Perfessor Greevey, like a bite to eat or drink?" With the kitchen clearly closed down for the night, this was indeed an astonishing offer.

"Nothing at all, thank you, Ebenezer," replied

Professor Greevey. "I was, of course, preparing to retire when you came in." He stood up, but then hesitated a moment and produced another piano-toothed smile. "I might say that you gentlemen were out rather late, were you not? What do you suppose could have drawn you out in such weather as this?"

"Well, we had to go out in the wag—" Lucky began importantly, finally finding an opportunity to slip his penny's worth into this conversation. A swift dig in the ribs from Neezer, however, put an instant end to the venture.

"What Lucky's meaning is that one of the wagons required fixing, and we was out fixing it," said Neezer. "It's needed in the morning for collecting ice from the *Silver Queen*. We was down there, trying it out, in a manner of speaking."

"Oh yes, trying it out, of course," replied Professor Greevey smoothly. "So the *Silver Queen* is in, is she? I presume that's where you found the boy?"

"The boy?" said Neezer, startled. It took him a moment to remember what boy was being referred to. "Oh no, Perfessor Greevey, not from the *Silver Queen*. He's . . . he's . . . my sister's boy. We collected *him* this night as well. It's *another* thing we was doing, you might say."

"You might indeed!" agreed Professor Greevey. "But I never knew you had a sister in the area." He paused, then shrugged. "Of course, why should I know about that?"

"Well, I *do* have a sister, anyhow," said Neezer, a trifle sullenly. This continued effort at being the cordial innkeeper was clearly beginning to wear thin. "The boy's to be apprenticed here."

"How . . . fortunate for him," replied Professor Greevey in a manner showing that "*un*fortunate" was more what he had in mind.

He crossed the room and started up the stairs, then hesitated again. "By the way, Ebenezer, perhaps if you provided more light in the rooms, your guests might not need to provide their own reading lanterns. Just a suggestion, of course. Well, good night, gentlemen!"

"Good night, Perfessor!" chorused the two gentlemen, after which the shadowy room was plunged into silence. But when the soft footfalls creeping up the stairs faded away, the men quickly removed their slickers and slid into two of the chairs pulled up to a table. Taddy was left standing behind them, for all the world forgotten again.

"Light! I'll give him light!" Neezer snarled under his breath.

"You think what he was doing was reading that book like he told us, Neezer?" Lucky asked.

"Oh, I expect he was doing that, all right," said Neezer. "But he could of been doing that in his cozy rooms upstairs now, couldn't he? What's he mean deciding to park hisself down here till all hours?"

Lucky hunched his shoulders and drew closer to Neezer. "Spying on us, maybe?"

"What for?" asked Neezer.

Lucky shrugged. "'Cause maybe he's got suspicions 'bout what we was doing tonight?"

Neezer weighed this suggestion carefully. "Never had 'em before." He weighed the question again. "No, don't think so. Anyway, supposing he found out something. What's he got in mind to do about it?"

Lucky scratched his head. "Blab on us?"

"What good's blabbing on us going to do for him?" said Neezer. "Nothing, that's what. There's no price on our heads nor nothing like that. I expect as how he's no more'n just plain nosy."

A few moments of deep silence followed this profound observation. It was finally broken by Lucky. "Well, I don't like him much anyways, Neezer."

"Well, nor do I," said Neezer. "Never have all them years he's been here. Light! I'll light *him,* I will!"

"Whyn't you tell him his rooms is spoke for?" asked Lucky. "In another manner o' speaking, Neezer, invite him to shove off."

Now, if looks could ever be said to kill, Lucky might have found himself flat on the floor with hands folded over a lily. "You got bats in your upstairs?" Neezer glared at him. "Perfessor Greevey's got connections what pay *him,* so he can pay *us* for all them rooms what occupies the top floor. And pays handsome, if you need to be reminded. I ain't anywhere close to inviting him to shove off. It appears, Lucky, you can't remember for more'n three minutes the motto of the Dog's Tail, which is them what pays, stays."

"Aw, can so," said Lucky.

Another silence descended upon the two men. Then Neezer began rubbing his chin. "You notice him asking about the *Silver Queen* again?"

"You brung it up first, Neezer," mumbled Lucky, his feelings clearly still smarting.

"And he pounced on it," said Neezer. "Every year, it's the *Silver Queen* he looks out for. Why? He ain't in the ice business."

"Ain't he friends with the cap'n?" asked Lucky. "I seen 'em going 'board ship together."

"For dinner, more'n likely." Neezer shrugged. "Nothing in that."

"What was you hoping for?" asked Lucky.

Neezer raised an eyebrow. "Oh, maybe I was hoping to get something on the old perfessor. Never hurts to get ourselves pertected, Lucky."

"You mean so we can have a big stick over him, like we got a stick over . . ." Lucky jerked a thumb over his shoulder in Taddy's direction.

Since the question asked about him by Professor Greevey, Taddy could have been a grease spot on the floor for all the notice paid him. This was the first sign he had been given that they were bearing in mind the fact that he was standing behind them. Did they not mind that he heard everything they were saying?

But on second thought, why should they? There was nothing in their low-voiced gruntings and growlings that he did not already know, at least nothing that made any difference. And he could never tell about any of it because of what they knew about *him*. It was what Lucky meant by "a big stick."

And it was why Taddy was standing there with his legs growing numb, nearly dead from bumps and bruises, weariness, and lack of sleep. He could easily have dropped onto the floor and, with his ragged bundle as his pillow, fallen soundly asleep. Yet he was too frightened even to do that.

Then all at once he felt a small prickle of anger. And another one, much larger. And yet another even larger than that. The Dog's Tail, no matter how dismal it looked outside, did provide food and rooms. And Taddy had been promised a nice place to sleep and good meals. Should he not be in his room right now in his own warm bed, with a breakfast of cooked oats covered with sugar and warm cream, griddle cakes, and two rashers of bacon awaiting him in the morning? Neezer and Lucky had made a bargain with him, and they had just better keep it. Because when you considered it, the stick they had over him was, after all, no bigger than the one he had over them! He would remind them of that. He *would*. And— and right now!

"Please, sirs."

Neezer and Lucky went right on talking.

"P-please, sirs," repeated Taddy.

The conversation at the table came to a sudden stop. The heads of the two men swiveled slowly in Taddy's direction. With glaring eyes dead-bolted to Taddy, Neezer allowed a few deadly moments of silence to pass before he spoke.

"Well, what is it you want?" This was in a tone of voice a far cry from the one reserved for honored paying guests of the Dog's Tail.

"P-p-please, sirs," said Taddy, "could-could I be shown to my room now, so I may unpack my belongings and go to bed?"

The two heads slowly swiveled back until their eyes met. Both men were grinning.

"Sirs? My, my, appears as how we got a gentleman in our midst," Neezer said. "Also appears as how we been forgetting our dooty. Now, supposing you just take him to his room right away." He relit the lantern and handed it to Lucky. Lucky then rose from the table in a leisurely manner, stretched, and then jerked his head to indicate that Taddy was to follow him.

Now, since Professor Greevey had risen *up* the stairs to his room, and a face in a nightcap had peered *down* the same stairs, it appeared that that was where the residents' rooms ought to be. Instead of making his way to these stairs, however, Lucky headed back toward the kitchen. Could there have been a set of stairs coming into the kitchen that Taddy had not seen? Or perhaps there was a room off the kitchen whose door he had missed.

But the kitchen, when they entered it, produced neither of these things. What Lucky pointed to was simply the gaping black hole under a table shoved in between the stove and outside wall. "There it is. That's yer place."

"B-b-but that's not a room," stammered Taddy.

"Looky here, *Toady,* nobody what I know of promised *rooms.* What you got promised was a warm place to sleep, 'n' that's what's there. Outhouse is that way, if you chooses to make the trip." Lucky directed a thumb at the back door of the kitchen. "But don't go getting pecoolyar ideas 'bout running off whilst you're out there. Neezer's arms ain't got any shorter'n when he last made mention o' them."

With these comforting words, Lucky turned on his heels and vanished through the door, thus removing from the room both himself and every bit of light provided by the lantern. Taddy now stood alone in total darkness to find his way across the room as best he could.

But at least he was now, finally, going to be allowed to go to bed, never mind what kind of bed it was. Lucky might as well have saved his breath about Taddy's going back through the kitchen door and into the freezing night again—no matter *what* the reason. All he wanted to do was lie down someplace—anyplace—and be able to close his eyes. He began to inch his way around the room.

Feeling his way past a cupboard and the hulking iron stove, he finally reached his appointed destination. As the idea of unpacking his meager belongings, and finding a place to put them, had now vanished with the hope of having his own room, he shoved his bundle under the table. Leaving his jacket on because it was clear that the promised "warm place to sleep" was now as stony cold as the stove beside it, he crawled in after the bundle, dropped onto the hard floor on his stomach, and cradled his head in his arms. He could now go to sleep at last!

Suddenly, to one side, he heard a scratching, scrabbling sound from behind the wall. Was it mice? Or—or *rats*! Taddy's eyes flew open. Then, from the other side somewhere near his head, he heard an odd snuffling sound, as if from some other kind of animal. Was there a dog asleep under the table? The dog perhaps that had served as the model for the painting? Taddy was now deathly afraid to stay where he was, but equally afraid to crawl back out. He lay motionless, too frightened even to close his eyes again.

If he lived until morning, he would have to find a way to use the "big stick" he held over Neezer and Lucky. Yet had Neezer not said he was making arrangements to have everything gone from the storage shed? Would anyone *then* believe that anything had been stolen at all, especially if pointed out by a little ragamuffin of a boy? All he would succeed in doing would be to bring attention to the fact that here was an orphan ripe and ready to be plucked for the workhouse! Taddy saw his "big stick" growing smaller and smaller until, finally, it became no stick at all. He was Neezer's prisoner, and that was all there was to it.

As for ever finding his mysterious twin, how would he ever do that? He would have to have help, have to trust someone. But consider the people he had met thus far: the two villains who had captured him; a slippery gentleman calling himself a professor; and someone with a frightened little face in a nightcap, known as Mrs. Scrat. And it was not to be expected that the Dog's Tail could provide much better. There would be no one to be trusted, no one to be believed. *No one! No one! No one!*

These words whirling through his brain were the last Taddy remembered as his fight to keep awake ended. His weary eyes drifted shut. And he was asleep at last.

Chapter IV
Beetle

Shhhhh. Shhhhh. Shhhhh.

Warm, moist air brushed across Taddy's neck.
Shhhhh. Shhhhh. His eyes, heavy-lidded from a deep,
exhausted sleep, opened a crack, then drooped shut
again. Only to snap open a moment later when he groggily remembered that instead of seeing his familiar little
dresser, chair, and a small curtained window letting in the
pale, early morning light, he had seen nothing but a
bleak, cold gray wall pressed against his nose. Then he
shivered as all at once the memory of what had happened
to him the night before flooded over him.

Shhhhh. Shhhhh. The air continued brushing across
Taddy's neck, reminding him of something else—the dog!
He lay facing the wall, rigid with fright. But the warm air
went on blowing gently, on and on until at last Taddy
turned his head and peeked cautiously over his shoulder.
Yes, there was something there indeed, but it was not
a dog!

Peering at him intently was a pair of enormous dark
eyes, made to seem even larger by being set in a pale,

pointy face. Altogether it had the sharp look of a weasel, while actually being the face of a small boy. The face backed away, but the eyes continued staring.

Taddy quickly sat up. "Who . . . who are you?"

The boy wiggled backward into the corner formed by the stove and the wall, never taking his eyes off Taddy. "I might ask likewise of you, and got a better right to know, cornsidering the small point that you have inwaded my bed. Wiv me in it, I should like to add!"

"I-I-I'm sorry," stammered Taddy. "But I was told to sleep here by . . . by Mr. Lucky. I didn't get to choose."

The boy's eyes narrowed as he weighed this explanation. "Well, I expect as how you didn't, no more than I did. But seems almighty queer that I never did hear anyfing as you were taking up residence last night."

"Perhaps it's because I didn't make any noise when I crawled in," Taddy said. "Then when I heard the dog under the table with me . . . I mean, I *thought* it was a dog . . . I never moved at all. It . . . it could have been the dog in the picture, you know." This last bit of information was added by Taddy to impress his listener with what might have been a gravely dangerous situation.

Far from being impressed, however, the boy rolled his eyes, clutched his stomach, and dissolved in silent laughter. "Where'd *you* come from? You sound like a raving ninny, you do! Do you think *any* dog would let you come creeping in and not come around to inwestigate? And if it had been the dog in the picter, you'd of been mincemeat. Good luck for you he's dead and gone."

The boy, of course, was absolutely right. Only a dog near death, or at the very least too ill to move, would have remained curled in his corner upon Taddy's arrival. And if that were the case, Taddy would not have had much to worry about. He could think of nothing to say, for he knew he had indeed been a prize ninny.

To Taddy's immense relief, the boy chose not to pursue the subject. "Wot's your name?" he asked abruptly.

"It's Taddy. But they say I'm to be called Toady. They say there's something here that skitters, so I'm to be something that hops. That's what a toad does," explained Taddy.

The boy gave a sigh of disgust. "I *know* wot a toad does. But for your information, a beetle's the warmint wot skitters, and happens Beetle's the name they dropped on *me*."

"Do you mind it?" asked Taddy.

"Can't say I do mind it. Anyway, around here you don't get to choose your name no more than you get to choose where you rest at night. Liking or not liking means nuffing at the Dog's Tail unless you're a paying customer."

"I know," said Taddy.

"How'd you know that already?" the boy, now known to be Beetle, returned fiercely.

"Because of how nice Mr. Neezer and Mr. Lucky were to someone named Professor Greevey last night," explained Taddy. "It was when we came into the big room with the dog's picture in it."

"Which room is knowed as the tavern, ninny," said Beetle. "You really do know nuffing about nuffing. Where'd you state that you come from? You never did bovver to reply to my question."

Taddy had never considered that the question delivered earlier had required an answer, because it had been left behind so quickly. He was certain, though, that there was nothing to be gained by mentioning this. Anyway, what was more important was choosing what he should tell about himself. *Be careful! Trust no one!* The words raced through his head again. "Not from the city. From . . . from way out in the country," he replied. There, *that* was safe enough.

"I guessed somefing like that!" Beetle sniggered. Then his eyes suddenly narrowed. "Wot they got on you?" he shot out.

"I . . . I . . ." Taddy began, but words froze in his throat. *Be careful! Trust no one!* He must not give out too much.

"Look here," said Beetle. "Nobody gets dumped under a table in the middle of night 'cause it's wot they asked from the wish fairy. They got somefing on you. You can tell me or not as you choose, but I'll find out anyhow. Besides, wot'll it hurt you to tell me? You got nuffing I want."

"Nuffing" indeed! "Nuffing" except perhaps being under Beetle's thumb forever and a day. Still, if he could find out anyway, and there was little reason to believe he could not, Taddy might as well tell him what he wanted to know. But—*be careful.*

"My aunt and uncle died," he said.

"So wot's that got to do wiv anyfing?" asked Beetle. "Lots of people got aunts and uncles, and cousins as well, wot died."

"But I *lived* with mine," exclaimed Taddy.

"Wot happened wiv your ma and pa?" Beetle asked.

"They died a long time ago . . . when I was a baby . . .

in New York." Well, that was the story Taddy had grown up with, and that was the story he would stick with.

"So, if I ain't mistaken, you've been made an orphin twicet, and a ripe subjeck for the workhouse," Beetle said. Then he fell silent, though it was certain that his brain was busily engaged in making further calculations.

"Ho! Now I got it!" he cried gleefully. "The workhouse being a place nobody desires to go, what I'm guessing is that Neezer offered you a one-way ticket in that direction if you ain't agreeable to placing yourself in the tender care of the Dog's Tail. And no need to confess. I can see by your face I got it right. Hoo! Hoo! Hoo!"

While Beetle chortled at his own cleverness, Taddy's insides did a somersault at the thought that he was now indeed in the clutches of yet another resident of this treacherous inn. But then all at once it struck him that if Neezer and Lucky had something on *him,* was it not likely that they also had something on Beetle? Why else would *he* be residing under a kitchen table at the Dog's Tail? This could hardly have been the work of a wish fairy either!

"Well . . . well . . ." Taddy swallowed hard. "What do they have on *you,* then?"

A look of shock and surprise wiped away the grin on Beetle's face. It was evident he had not expected such a sharp-witted question from someone he classed as a ninny. But just at that moment, there was the sound of the kitchen door opening and footsteps scurrying across the room.

"Sssssst!" Beetle hissed. "Here's Mrs. Scrat!" Then, in a menacing whisper, he added something that made it very clear he had no intention of ever answering Taddy's question. "Now, see here, there's three rules you best remember. Rule one's that I'm the one wot was here first, so I get first choice of everyfing. Rule two's that you better quit with that *Mr.* Neezer and likewise *Mr.* Lucky stuff, lest it pleases their fancy and they take to requiring it of *me*. Plain *Neezer* and *Lucky's* good enough. Last rule, and most important, is remembering which side is which under the table—this being mine and that being yours. Don't ever, ever let me catch you touching my stuff wot's hanging there on the wall behind, nor anyfing else belonging to me!"

Beetle jerked a grimy thumb at what Taddy had thought was no more than rags hanging from nails on the wall, but now was recognized as a filthy, ragged jacket and another pitiful piece of clothing that might pass for a shirt.

"Where do I put my own things?" asked Taddy. He wondered if rule three applied to Beetle as well, but strongly suspected it did not.

"On the wall like me, if someone gets around to perwiding the nails. Where else did you think, in your own nice little cupboard?" Beetle shook his head in disbelief. "And maybe someone will also perwide you a bed cover, but you don't go touching mine anyhow." He shoved yet another ratty piece of something into the corner as he snatched his jacket from the wall and started to wiggle swiftly out from the table. "Now move along. We got stuff to do."

"What?" asked Taddy, crawling after him.

"Everyfing," replied Beetle over his shoulder. "You

got a name for it, we get to do it. Morning, Mrs. Scrat! This here's Toady, who you no doubt's heard about."

To Taddy's surprise, the tiny woman enveloped in a drab brown apron, with mouse-colored hair untidily pinned to the top of her head, was indeed the owner of the same face that had peered over the stair railing into the tavern the night before. Neezer's overblown politeness must positively have been only to impress Professor Greevey, for it appeared that she was no more than a servant at the Dog's Tail. Her face, which still managed to look as if it expected something dreadful to happen momentarily, produced a dim smile at the introduction.

The smile, however, vanished almost before it had registered with Taddy. For Mrs. Scrat, with apron flying, was now directing all her attention toward hoisting herself up and swinging her little legs onto the worktable at the center of the kitchen. Then, standing on the very tips of her toes, she reached precariously upward to lift from the ceiling hooks an enormous black fry pan and a sauce pot so heavy it very nearly toppled her right off the table. Taddy stood hypnotized by this curious performance, until he felt a sudden, sharp jerk on his arm.

"No need to gawk. She ain't ever tipped over yet," said Beetle. His tone of voice showed how superior he felt that he could report this to the new boy.

"Oh dear!" Mrs. Scrat, now safely back on the floor, wrung her hands nervously. "Haven't you boys gone yet? You *must hurry!*" She looked as if she were going to cry. "And you'll tell Toady what's to be done, won't you, Beetle?"

"Never fear, Mrs. Scrat. I'll tell him, all right." A slight swagger now appeared in Beetle's walk as he headed for the back door. And no wonder! By putting Taddy in his charge, Mrs. Scrat had firmly established that Beetle was no longer the lowest rung on the servant ladder. He had suddenly become head boy, and would have been, it seemed, even if he had not pried loose information that already placed Taddy firmly under his thumb.

"You know who Mrs. Scrat is, I expect," Beetle said out of the side of his mouth, although patently expecting no such thing.

"She's . . . she's the cook, isn't she?" replied Taddy as soon as the kitchen door closed behind them.

"Ha! More'n that," said Beetle. "So happens she is also married to Mr. Scrat. That means nuffing to you, I suppose?"

Taddy shook his head. For other than the fact that Mrs. Scrat was not also the Widow Scrat, this revelation did not seem very remarkable to him.

"Well, for your information," Beetle said, "Mr. Scrat is Neezer, one and the same, which makes Mrs. Scrat out to be Mrs. Neezer. Now, how do you feel about *that*?"

How Taddy felt was as if something heavy had dropped into the pit of his stomach. For even though he had not had much time to review it, Mrs. Scrat *had* given him a smile. And faint and fleeting though it was, it was the first smile he had had in days, and certainly unexpected from anyone at the Dog's Tail. Now this first and only glimmer of friendliness had been snatched away.

The smile must have been a careless mistake at best, but more likely a false one meant to disarm him. Funny little Mrs. Scrat now shown to be the wife of Neezer! *Be careful! Trust no one!* Those words became more ominous with every person Taddy met. He must never let down his guard and forget them for a single moment!

In the meantime, the very look on Taddy's face must have been enough to satisfy Beetle that his point had been made about Mrs. Scrat's importance, for he now turned his attention elsewhere.

"This here's our first chore," he said, nodding to a stack of logs piled up against the wall, "wood for the stove for breakfast. Eight trips is what it takes most times." He paused, looking slyly at Taddy. "But things being a mite changed now, as is plain for all to see, why I'll be doing one trip and then be helping Mrs. Scrat whilst you lug the rest."

This instruction, plainly invented by Beetle, was a wonderfully clear picture of how the land was to lie from then on. But if there were any remaining doubt about this, it was immediately dispelled. "This here's the outhouse," he announced. "My turn first!"

When he reappeared, dancing about and flapping his arms from the cold, he was ready to continue his travelogue. "Over yonder is where Neezer keeps anyfing he's not likely to want the world to know about, which is just about everyfing." Beetle jerked his head in the direction of the shed with the double padlocks with which Taddy was all too familiar. "And that other place behind it," Beetle went on, "you'll more'n likely be interdooced to before the day is ended. It's the icehouse. Mostly stores ice. Sometimes stores me as well."

"Y-y-you?" stammered Taddy with horror. For in the gloomy half light of early morning he could see that the ugly little building, the one with which he was also sadly familiar from the night before, had no windows. Not one!

So it must have been not only freezing inside, but frighteningly dark as well. "You . . . you get *stored* in there?" said Taddy. "What . . . whatever for?"

"Whatever for? Well, for when I've done somefing I oughtn't. *That's* whatever for." Beetle gave a careless shrug and began to load his arms with the firewood.

"But how long do you stay there?" asked Taddy.

"Oh, until I've learned my lesson, which means however long Neezer thinks it takes." Beetle's pinched face managed to produce a crafty grin. "Thing is, soon as ever I get unfroze in the warm kitchen, the lesson gets forgot."

"But what if they leave you in the icehouse too long, and you never do unfreeze?" Taddy asked.

"Not likely they'd ever do that," Beetle replied. "I'm too waluable, cornsidering as how they get my undiwided attention, and pay nuffing for it."

"Yes, but what if . . . what if they put you in there and forget all about you one day?" persisted Taddy.

"There's always that now, ain't there," said Beetle coolly, and disappeared into the house.

Chapter V
Scrat's Ice and Odd Jobs

By the time Taddy had stumbled into the kitchen with his seventh load of logs, the cracks around the doors of the iron stove already glowed red from a fire blazing within. The smells of bread baking in the oven, porridge bubbling in the pot, and bacon sizzling in the great black frying pan all mingled deliciously in the warm room, giving notice that "good meals served regular" was at least something that had not turned out to be one of Neezer's big lies.

Taddy had eaten nothing in nearly a day and a half, and the tantalizing aromas were almost more than he could bear. But it was certain that in only a few minutes his earlier thoughts of a grand breakfast would become real. It did not even bother him that Beetle's idea of "helping Mrs. Scrat" appeared to be simply leaning against the table watching her beat up batter for muffins, offering his "undiwided" attention but not much else.

"Now then, here's Toady with the last of the wood," said Mrs. Scrat, thumping her spoon against the bowl.

"And mighty slow about it cornsidering the time now

showing on the clock, if I might be allowed an observation, Mrs. Scrat," said Beetle.

"You might," allowed Mrs. Scrat, "but it's only his first day. He'll do better," she added with another fading smile at Taddy. Then her eyes suddenly flew open in a look of shock and dismay. "Oh dear, whatever have I been thinking of letting you dawdle about, Beetle! You should have been setting the tables. Oh my!"

"No fear, Mrs. Scrat," replied Beetle. "Wiv the two of us, it won't take any time at all." He ambled toward the door leading to the tavern, motioning Taddy to follow.

Taddy was certain it would end up more like the one of *him* rather than the two of *them* doing anything, once out of sight of Mrs. Scrat. But to his surprise, once in the tavern, Beetle darted to a chest at one side of the room and began furiously snatching up handfuls of tarnished forks, knives, and spoons from a drawer. Then he shoved some into Taddy's hands.

"You know how to set a table, I presume," he said loftily, and flew over to the nearest table, where he began slamming down the said forks, knives, and spoons. This activity was followed by the setting of plates, bowls, and cups and saucers with near lightning speed. It was certainly a very different Beetle from the one who had just departed from the kitchen. But Taddy was soon able to discover why.

The tavern had already begun to fill with customers. And at a table by the door, collecting money, sat Neezer and Lucky. Although they gave no sign of having seen either Beetle or Taddy, there was no doubt that their late arrival and everything they were doing was being recorded for future use in the collective brains of the two men. They also recorded the arrival of Mrs. Scrat, who scurried back and forth from kitchen to serving table with bowls of steaming porridge, large pitchers of milk, hot coffee and tea, jars of sugar, dishes of butter, and platters heaped with bacon, rolls, and muffins. The men soon made round trips to the serving table, plates spilling with food, which they went right to work shoveling into their mouths. They only paused long enough to collect money as another patron straggled in.

With only one exception, the whole lot of these were rough seamen and dockside workers, with bearded faces beaten and scarred by harsh weather and by violent acts that could only be guessed. They were hardly faces to give Taddy any reason to feel more cheerful about his future. The exception to the rest was the man seated alone by the far corner window. He was delicately applying butter to a small bit of roll with long, bony fingers, while at the same time never removing his eyes from a book lying open by his plate. This man, however, was perhaps more chilling than the rest, for it was none other than Professor Greevey.

But at the moment, Taddy had a more pressing matter on his mind. For the room was now thick with the clinking and clattering of cutlery and dishes, and the grunting and chewing of the otherwise largely silent patrons of the Dog's Tail who, aside from Professor Greevey, seemed grimly bent on getting their money's worth. And as the two boys scrambled back and forth answering the gruff commands of "Fetch me a roll!" or "I want more tea!" (with never so much as one "please" to be heard), Taddy watched with sinking spirits and a further shrinking stomach all food and drink rapidly disappearing from pitchers, platters, and bowls on the serving table.

"Don't we get to eat now?" Taddy whispered to Beetle.

"Eat *now*? Who do you think we are, Neezer's royal guests?" Beetle's eyes rolled heavenward. "We eat whenever everyone else gets finished—*total* finished—and not one minute before that."

"But couldn't we just have a small bite of something now?" persisted Taddy.

Beetle shrugged. "All depends which you walue most, a small bite of bacon . . . or your life. You get to choose."

To no one's surprise, Taddy chose to wait until the meal was officially over and the tavern empty but for Neezer and Lucky, huddled in conversation at their table, and Taddy and Beetle.

"Now," said Beetle, "we eat!"

Eat? Eat *what*? There was nothing left in the serving dishes but a scraping of oatmeal, a film of grease on the bacon platter, and crumbs on the tray that once held rolls and muffins. But the question was soon answered when Taddy saw Beetle snatch up a half-eaten roll left on someone's plate and jam it into his mouth. This was followed by a small, ragged piece of muffin from the same source, all washed down by a swallow of someone's leftover tea. And the whole act was performed as Beetle was stacking dishes from a table.

Scraps! That is what they were left to eat. Scraps that might have been fed to the ugly dog whose picture hung on the wall. So this was one of the "good meals" promised by Neezer! Still, with no other promises kept, why should this one be any different? Taddy, however, had no intention of eating such food. He would *not*! They could not make him do it.

"You going to be picky picky?" asked Beetle, his cheeks puffed from whatever he had just thrown in his mouth. "You might as well be adwised, the menu ain't going to get any better. And I don't know about most indiwiduals, but I don't fare too well wivout food and drink."

Taddy, athough never having tried it, was certain he would not do too well either. And if it was true that the food was not going to get any better, it was also true that he was not going to get any less hungry. Hesitantly, he reached for a crust of bread lying on a greasy plate. Trying not to think of where it had come from or who had last bitten into it, he put it slowly into his mouth. A moment later, he was jamming into the same location every morsel of food he could find. He was so intent on snatching up a crust from a roll that he never noticed anyone approaching him until he was grabbed roughly by the scruff of his neck.

"All right there, boy," barked Neezer, being the one who had Taddy by the neck, "let's pay more notice to carrying dishes to the kitchen than carrying grub to your face."

"Toady should watch as how Beetle does it, shouldn't he, Neezer?" said Lucky.

"We-e-ell, more nor less," replied Neezer sourly, thus putting a sudden end to the grin that was developing on Beetle's face. "But I am informing all present that regardless of whether deserving or not, Beetle has now got hisself up a step in life, in a manner of speaking."

Beetle's eyes flew open, and his jaw went limp. The grin quickly returned. "A . . . a step up?"

"Keeping in mind it's only in a manner of speaking," Neezer shot back. "But you'll be coming alongside of me to the docks, fetching ice off the *Silver Queen* and other visits of a business nature."

"But what 'bout me? Who's going to be a-helping of me?" whined Lucky.

"You get Toady," replied Neezer, "and no more said about it."

"Rats!" said Lucky.

Taddy could not see where being transferred as a workhorse from Lucky to Neezer was any kind of improvement in life, one being as bad as the other. But Beetle's chest was visibly puffed out. He threw Taddy a look of triumph. Well, to be sure, if Neezer had said this was a step up, then who could argue it? And it was certainly the final seal (as if one were really needed) on Beetle's position as first boy.

"Well, hop along then, Toady, you've stuffed yourself long enough," Lucky grumbled. He picked up two plates and slammed them down onto the pile Taddy was collecting.

A few moments ago, Taddy could hardly bear to touch the remains of someone's breakfast, much less eat them. Now he looked longingly at whatever little bits and pieces still clung to plates and bowls. His stomach felt at least three quarters empty as he stumbled out to the kitchen. With his hands still scraped and sore from carrying the rough logs, his arms bruised and his legs aching, it seemed that his whole new life was made up of being loaded down with one thing or another and told to lug it someplace else. What would it be next? he wondered. And he soon found out.

As the all-important Beetle strutted off with Neezer, Taddy followed a disgusted Lucky through the back door on a trail that led right to the ugly little windowless building, now known to be the icehouse. In front of it there stood a small wagon that was not the same one Taddy had traveled in the night before, for this one had words painted on either side—SCRAT'S ICE AND ODD JOBS.

"And what you got to do now, case you haven't figgered it out," growled Lucky, "is move what's in there and put it in over there." A fat, dirty thumb jerked in one direction, then another.

Ice! Heavy, slippery cakes of ice! Ice to be lugged from the icehouse and loaded onto the wagon—that was Taddy's next job. And all made worse by remembering what Beetle had told him about being "stored" there. How must it feel to be locked in a small room, the door tightly locked, and surrounded by icy darkness? What had Beetle done to deserve such a terrible punishment? The miserable trips back and forth from icehouse to wagon could not end soon enough for Taddy.

At last, however, he finally found himself perched precariously on the front seat of the wagon, heading out into the alley. Beside him hunched the glowering, deadly silent Lucky, furious because Taddy kept dropping the heavy cakes of ice and could only carry the very smallest ones.

"Not like Beetle," Lucky muttered, "who got muscles somewhat better'n a flea." Beetle's stock at the Dog's Tail was indeed rising even further as Taddy's continued to sink.

But Taddy soon had something else to think about

beside trips to the icehouse, or how much more miserable life would be under a Beetle with head puffed up beyond all reason. For Taddy had suddenly realized that he was venturing out into the city in broad daylight, sitting atop a wagon where he was displayed for all the world to see. How curious it was that he actually felt safer at the Dog's Tail! At least there, for the moment, his life did not appear to be in danger. *Danger!* Was that not the very word his Uncle Buntz had used? Where in the city did it lie? Around which corner? Taddy drew his chin down deep into his collar, trying to hide as much of his face as possible.

For while it had been all but deserted the night before, now the dockside was alive with sailors crawling over the ships, dock workers loading and unloading cargo, and numbers of scruffy children playing dangerously in between everyone's legs. Could one of these children turn out to be a boy Taddy's age, with the same straight sandy-brown hair and the same gray-blue eyes? Might he be Taddy's *twin*? Was there something about being twins that was where the mysterious danger lay? When a boy stopped to look curiously at the wagon, Taddy stiffened and pulled his chin down even more deeply into his collar. *Be careful!* No matter what, *be careful*!

The sour and sullen Lucky remained sunk in his own angry thoughts and never bothered to issue a warning when the wagon rumbled around the corner onto the cobblestones. He barely shifted his head when the unsuspecting Taddy was very nearly pitched out onto the street. Could anyone on that street have guessed how frightened and miserable he was, hanging on to a hard, bumping, thumping wooden bench for his very life, while keeping his face buried in his collar for the same reason?

But the street was much too intent on its own affairs to care about a young boy bouncing atop a delivery wagon. Some shopkeepers were busy bringing out meats and vegetables and dried fruits from storage rooms. Others were arranging trays of buttons and laces and bright red, blue, and green ribbons in shop windows. Shoppers, some stopping to chat with friends, were already out with their baskets. From behind the windows of houses, children peeked through lace curtains at all the hustle and bustle. Through some windows, mops danced mysteriously amidst clouds of dust, wielded by diligent young parlor maids. The SCRAT'S ICE AND ODD JOBS wagon was simply a part of the busy scene. Who was there to pay it any attention?

Bump! Thump! The wagon pulled around another corner, leaving the cobblestones behind, and drew to a stop. It was then that Lucky chose to speak, or rather snarl, as was more truly the case.

"Now see here, Toady, as you has no doubt noticed, we has stopped. First, get your face out o' that collar and quit staring ahead like you seen a spook. Gives me the living creeps, it does." Lucky paused to give his nose a swipe on the cuff of his jacket.

"What we does now," he then went on, "is deliver two cakes of ice to the icebox of this house belonging to a party name of Brown. Which name makes no matter to you on account o' you ain't going to be talking to anyone. I answers everything, and all that comes out o' you is 'no, Lucky' or 'yes, Lucky.' Other ways you just keep your trap shut. And bear in mind all what Neezer told you 'bout them long arms he got, case you get any ideas. Is I making myself clear, Toady?"

Taddy nodded. It was all very clear, indeed! But Lucky might as well have saved his breath—most of it at any rate. In every house but two that they entered, Taddy was simply Scrat's delivery boy. He could have been Lucky's shadow for all the interest paid him.

Taddy, on his part, was just as happy *not* to be noticed. After all, the fewer people who noticed him the better. Safely "invisible" inside the houses, he felt free to look with envy around the warm cheerful kitchens they entered, with their bright red and blue curtains, shiny copper pans, and sturdy pottery dishes neatly piled on the shelves. How it all reminded him of the cozy kitchen he himself had grown up in!

"Why, wherever is Beetle? And who might you be, young man?" This question, the very first showing that anyone had noticed Taddy's presence, so startled him that at first he could only stand stupidly and stare.

The question came from a short, plump woman in a pink print calico dress very nearly hidden by a voluminous, sparkling white apron. Her enormous mobcap framed a face with the rosiest cheeks Taddy had ever seen in his life. Five small, wide-eyed children with equally rosy cheeks clustered like so many towheaded stair steps around her skirt. But the kindliness in her voice completely drove from Taddy's mind the warnings Lucky had given him, or even the warnings he had given himself.

"I . . . I'm . . ." he began shyly.

"This here's Toady, Mrs. Diggles," interrupted Lucky, throwing Taddy a murderous look. "Now, ain't that right, Toady?"

"Y-y-yes, Lucky," quavered Taddy.

Mrs. Diggles looked from one to the other, but reserved any opinions she had to herself. "Well," she said briskly, "nothing is needed today, Lucky. I would like you to stop back tomorrow, however. But perhaps I could interest Toady in a nice, fresh-baked cookie?" She nodded toward a table heaped with breads and cookies and all manner of delicious-looking baked goods intended, no doubt, for sale in Diggles's Bakery, which occupied the front of the house where the family lived.

Almost before Taddy could blink, Lucky jumped in. "Begging your pardon, ma'am, but it ain't allowed. Toady's et his dinner, and anything more'd likely spoil a boy's supper, which ain't generally good for his health."

Well, neither Mrs. Diggles nor anyone else could argue a splendid rule like this. That is, not unless Taddy were free to report that his "dinner" had been one hard crust of bread grudgingly handed him by Lucky from a dirty sack, plus one sip of weak tea from an equally dirty bottle. Or that his supper would, without much doubt, equal what had been provided for breakfast.

But as they prepared to leave, Lucky suddenly turned to Mrs. Diggles with a sly smile. "Howsumever, ma'am, it don't seem right to keep the lad from a nice cookie such as yer bakery pervides. Whyn't you just give one"—he reconsidered—"or two of 'em to me. I'll keep 'em safe until after he's et his supper."

With Lucky standing there holding out his hand, Mrs. Diggles had little choice but to give him the cookies, which he promptly stuffed into his pocket.

"Now, see that he gets them," said Mrs. Diggles, a request that she doubtless knew would never be met.

"Oh, I will, Mrs. Diggles, ma'am," replied Lucky soulfully.

All Mrs. Diggles could do was offer Taddy a warm smile as they left, a smile that Taddy was too frightened even to return.

Chapter VI
A Twin Discovered!

Softly fluttering lights had begun to appear behind windows, offering a brief glimpse from time to time of cozy parlors with children at play and dining rooms with tables being set for the evening meal. But outside, under the cold, darkening sky, the wagon bearing the sign SCRAT'S ICE AND ODD JOBS continued to rumble up and down the city streets.

Was it really still afternoon? Taddy wondered. Would this day never end? Though it seemed impossible to imagine, he found himself actually longing to return to the Dog's Tail! Never mind a miserable supper of scraps. Never mind a bed that was no more than a hard floor under a table. And never even mind that he would be back together with a Beetle made even more impossible by today's proceedings. But the Dog's Tail was warm at least. And now, with the coming of evening, the chilling wind had turned fiercer and stronger, seeming to bite its way right through to Taddy's bones.

He was so cold that his only interest when the wagon drew to yet another stop was the few minutes he would have in a warm kitchen before they rolled on. His hands felt frozen and as stiff as icicles as he stood shivering at the back of the wagon, waiting as Lucky rounded the bend, flapping his arms. From the look on his face, Taddy expected that he would be receiving yet another lecture not much different from the others delivered at every stop after they had left Diggles's Bakery.

He was right, excepting that this one began with Lucky grabbing him roughly by the collar, then yanking him forward so their faces were almost touching. Lucky's eyes glared.

"You got firmly in your head what I been telling you, Toady?"

Taddy nodded as best he could, considering that his face was right up against Lucky's nose.

"Well," snarled Lucky, "if you know what's good for your health, you will partikalar remember it at *this* house. Nothing is to come out o' your mouth but 'yes, Lucky,' excepting it be 'no, Lucky.' No way, no time, no how! You think you got that final stuck in your bonnet?" A sharp jerk on the collar effectively cut off any nod attempted by Taddy.

But what was so different about this house that made Lucky's warnings more violent than the rest? The question was answered by only a quick glance. How he had failed to note it, Taddy could not imagine. For this house of solid red brick was enormous, perhaps three times as large as the very largest house they had stopped at all that day.

It was not just distinguished by its size, however. For a broad flight of curved brick steps led to a pair of tall, carved, double oak doors, graced by two-foot-tall gleaming brass lanterns. Every window that reached out from the doors was protected by black iron bars heavily ornamented with iron birds, leaves, and flowers, costly in themselves, but looking as if they protected things far more costly within. Another row of windows rose above, and these were capped by a slate roof with arched dormer windows that spoke of yet another level of rooms above. If any one word could be used to describe this house, it was surely the word *grand*.

What lay directly behind those tall doors, however, Taddy was not to discover that day. Instead, he and Lucky stumped up a dank side path that took them to a tradesman's entrance. There, in answer to a doorbell ring, they were let into a large, blindingly bright kitchen by a young maid in a starched white apron and cap. Her expression scarcely changed as Lucky announced himself.

"Scrat's," he said tersely.

"It's the ice and odd-jobs man, Mrs. Fry," announced the maid to a woman in a trim gray dress and crisp white apron, busy whipping up eggs in a large white enamel basin at the kitchen table.

"Well, run and tell Mrs. Mainyard. See if she wants any more than just the regular ice delivery for the icebox, or any special jobs done," replied Mrs. Fry.

While he and Lucky waited for this message to be delivered, Taddy was able to take account of the tall, glass-paned, white cabinets, the gleaming copper pots and pans reflecting the brilliant gaslight overhead, and a boy about his own size standing at the sink scrubbing the white porcelain counter. The boy turned to stare a moment at the new arrivals, but a look from Mrs. Fry had him quickly back attending to his task.

"All right, Jeremy," she said, "you can leave off with that and go tend to the sweeping job in the cellar. And please bring back an extra bucket of coal for the fireplace in the dining room when you're finished. But remember now, no dawdling!"

Jeremy, after a secret, sidelong look at the new arrivals, hurriedly disappeared through a door next to the stove. This was a boy who seemed to be in about the same position as Taddy at the Dog's Tail. But oh, how Taddy envied a boy destined to work in this bright, warm kitchen, wearing a nice, clean, blue flannel shirt and trousers. Furthermore, he did not appear to be a boy who was living off scraps and crusts of bread. It was difficult not to compare his day filled with food and warmth to Taddy's own, spent starving and shivering on an ice wagon.

But Taddy's attention was now taken up by the arrival in the kitchen of three people, a woman and two young girls, one around the age of ten or eleven, the other a little older. Both girls were dressed alike in royal blue velveteen dresses with large, white lace collars. There, however, the similarity ended, for the older one had hair as straight and dark as midnight tied back with a wide, white satin bow, while the younger girl wore a blue bow that barely restrained a mass of unruly golden curls. Further, the dark-haired girl stared at Taddy with bold eyes the color of green glass, while the second one peeked shyly at him with soft blue eyes, then quickly looked down.

As for the woman, Taddy dared only a quick glance at her, but it was enough for him to decide that she was the most beautiful person he had ever seen. Her hair, dark like that of the one young girl, was swept up into a knot held with a flashing circlet of diamonds. Her eyes also matched those of the girl, a brilliant green, and her cheeks were tinted the delicate pink of apple blossoms. At her pale, slender neck lay a brooch encrusted with more sparkling diamonds, fastening the high collar of her rustling black silk dress. This then must be Mrs. Mainyard, fetched by the young maid, and, thought Taddy, a truly fitting person to live in such a grand house.

"Yes, Lucky, thank you, we will take an extra cake or two of ice for the icehouse, if you have it," she said in a soft, sweet voice. "And I see that you have a different helper today. Is the other boy no longer with you?"

"If you're meaning Beetle, Mrs. Main'ard," replied Lucky, nervously shuffling from one foot to the other, "he's . . . he's off with Neezer."

"And"—Mrs. Mainyard hesitated, then smiled at Taddy—"where did you find your new helper? Is he from the town?"

Taddy felt his heart give a quick thump. What could it matter where he came from? *Be careful! Be careful!* And yet why think about being careful with the beautiful, smiling Mrs. Mainyard? He really was a prize ninny, just as Beetle had said! But the question was for Lucky, not for Taddy.

Lucky, however, appeared to have gone into shock with the effort of trying to remember where Taddy was supposed to have come from. After staring vacantly off into a corner of the room for several moments and chewing his lip for several more, he finally grinned. "He's Neezer's sister's boy, Mrs. Main'ard . . . name of Toady."

"I see," said Mrs. Mainyard, captivating Taddy with another smile. "Well, if you'll fetch the ice, I will meet you at the icehouse." She dipped a graceful hand into a pocket of her dress and drew out a ring of keys.

At the same moment, the hand of the dark-haired girl darted out and yanked a golden curl of the girl beside her. But it was the dark-haired girl who let out a yowl of pain.

"Mama!" she screamed. "Dora pulled my hair again!"

"Did you do that, Dora?" asked Mrs. Mainyard. "Did you pull Madelina's hair?"

But Dora did not burst out with an angry reply, as expected. She only lowered her head and stared dumbly at the floor.

"Well, then," said Mrs. Mainyard softly, "you must go to your room, Dora. When you are allowed out, you must tell Madelina you are sorry."

With a triumphant smile on her face, Madelina watched Dora trudge dejectedly from the room.

How unjust this was! Taddy wanted desperately to tell Mrs. Mainyard what had really happened. But "yes, Lucky" and "no, Lucky" were all the words that could come from his mouth. He had to remain silent and do nothing but follow Lucky from the kitchen.

After unloading ice from the wagon, they returned with it to the back of the house. There Mrs. Mainyard, enveloped in a rich, ermine-trimmed cape and hood, stood before the door of a small brick building with no windows and a heavily padlocked door. It looked like nothing more nor less than a little fortress. Mrs. Mainyard deftly unlocked the padlock, then waited while they carried in the ice. It seemed curious to Taddy that she should be the one tending to this instead of a servant, and even more curious that she should wait there for them to make yet another delivery. Lucky, however, never questioned this, so Taddy could only think that there was nothing so curious about it after all.

Then minutes later, something happened that drove all else from Taddy's mind—Dora's curls, Madelina's meanness, even the beautiful Mrs. Mainyard—everything! For as he and Lucky were leaving after delivering the order of ice for the great, solid-oak icebox in the kitchen, the boy Jeremy came through the cellar door with his bucket of coal. As he passed Taddy and Lucky, he looked directly into Taddy's face, and Taddy looked back at his. And Taddy's breath caught sharply in his throat.

For looking at him were gray-blue eyes like the eyes he had seen looking back at him from the small cracked mirror over his dresser for all of his life. And over the eyes was the same sandy-brown hair. Taddy quickly ducked his head and scurried after Lucky, his heart pounding. For he was absolutely certain that what he had just looked into was the face of his twin!

Chapter VII
Beetle's Confession

By the time the ice wagon pulled up behind the Dog's Tail, Taddy was numb with cold and weariness, yet his brain had never stopped spinning all the way back. His twin! A twin who was a servant boy just as Taddy was, only in much finer quarters. A twin who might be in as much danger as Taddy was himself! And how was it that no one there recognized how much they looked like one another? Had Jeremy noted it? Did *he* know he had a twin? Did he know about the danger they might both be in? How should Taddy behave when he returned to the Mainyard house? Oh, there was a great deal to be thought out. And *alone*!

"Where have you been?" Beetle asked him crossly the moment he appeared in the kitchen of the Dog's Tail, as if Taddy had anything to do with it. "You're late! Wot do you mean leaving me to do all the supper work?"

So once again, Taddy found himself racing around the tavern, with the only difference being that it was for supper rather than breakfast. He was soon warmed up, but so tired he could barely move his arms and legs. And worst of all, he felt as if his stomach were pressing right up against his backbone. The smells of roasted meat, brown sauce, muffins, and puddings were unbearable. So unbearable that as Taddy stood beside the serving table near the end of the meal, he snatched the one remaining muffin on the platter without thinking, and began stuffing it into his mouth.

"Uh-oh!" hissed Beetle. "Now you've done it!"

Too late, Taddy saw Neezer and Lucky crossing the room toward them.

"What kind of lessons you been teaching him today, Lucky?" Keeping his back carefully to the rest of the tavern patrons, Neezer grabbed Taddy's neck so roughly that Taddy nearly choked on the evidence, if evidence were needed to prove his wrongdoing.

"Well, I teached him to keep his mouth shut," replied Lucky piously.

"Not shut enough," snarled Neezer, grabbing the remainder of the muffin from Taddy's hand and slamming it back on the platter. "The rule around here's that no help eats till after the guests all been fed. Seems to me as how you minded that rule this morning, and now you've gone and disremembered it."

Neezer punctuated his speech with yet another shake of Taddy's neck. "So, it seems to me as how a little stay in the icehouse might keep everyone remembering as they ought. Ain't that right, Lucky?"

Before Lucky could reply, a small, timid voice coming from behind Taddy suddenly blurted out "Oh Mr. Scrat, not the icehouse already! He's only just come!"

"Your name Lucky, Mrs. Scrat?" Neezer growled under his breath. "Why don't you get back in the kitchen where you belong, and mind your own business?" He turned and flashed what was intended to be a smile at any patrons in the tavern who might be paying more attention to this scene than their supper. "Well, Lucky, what you standing there for? Take him away!"

Taddy was led away past Beetle, who was sporting an insolent grin on his face, at the same time leaving behind all hope of even the remains of roasted meat and thick brown sauce, muffin crumbs, or dabs of pudding. All he took with him was the knowledge that Mrs. Scrat's trembling smiles were not meant to deceive him. But how was a smile to help him in the dreaded icehouse?

He was taken right out and shoved into the icehouse without another word. The door was slammed behind him. The key was turned in the lock. And he was alone, imprisoned in the small, ugly building with no windows and no light, surrounded only by stacks of cold, cold, hard, hard ice.

How was it to be believed that in less than twenty-four hours he could have ended up here? What had he done that was so terrible? He had just taken one bite of muffin—a *muffin*! That was all. And now he was locked up in the icehouse. Perhaps to be forgotten? And to think that he actually thought himself "safe" at the Dog's Tail, that danger only lurked somewhere else in the city. If things were not so grim, the thought might produce a smile. For what could happen that would be more dangerous than the position Taddy was in now? And all for a bite of muffin!

And then Taddy thought of his twin, a twin who now had a name—Jeremy. Was the first sight Taddy had of him to be the last?

Jeremy! Muffin! Jeremy! Muffin! Taddy began saying the words out loud. Jeremy! Muffin! Then he hugged his arms about himself and began to hop up and down. Oh, how cold it was! J-Jeremy! M-muffin! His teeth were beginning to chatter. Up and down. Up and down. He was growing tireder and tireder. He could not feel his fingers anymore. His feet were numb. Up—and—down. Up—and—down. Up—and—down. Slower—slower. J-Jeremy! M-m-m-m-muffin! And with that last, Taddy fell to the ground in a heap. It was just as the door to the icehouse flew open.

Lucky stood there shaking his head in disgust. "Lying down already. You only been in here fifteen minutes, thanks to Neezer's kindly heart. Come on! Get up! We're going back in."

Late that night, when at last Taddy crawled wearily under the table, he found it impossible to fall asleep. Even after the Dog's Tail had grown dark and silent, with not a scratching, a scrabbling, or a whispering to be heard in the building, he still tossed and turned on the hard floor. Finally, thinking he might awaken the sleeping Beetle beside him, he ended up lying stiffly on his back, staring up at the bottom of the kitchen table.

Beetle was so soundly asleep, however, he hardly made a sound, not even of breathing. Sleep had come so easily to him, and no wonder, with his stomach full of food and no recent memories of a stay in the icehouse. The food was only scraps, to be sure, and no better than what would have been fed the dog, had he still been there. But it was still *food,* and how Taddy envied Beetle his full stomach and his sound sleep. For every time

Taddy closed his eyes, gnawing hunger and the feeling that he was back in the icehouse again caused his eyes to fly open.

Was it going to be like this forever? Having a big hole in his stomach where food ought to be? Being thrown into the icehouse for doing no more than taking a bite of muffin? And what if he were to do something a little worse? What kind of punishment would that bring? And once again came the same questions. Who was there to turn to? Who was there to trust? No one, that was who! No one! No one!

All at once, Taddy felt burning tears rolling down his cheeks. He quickly rolled over onto his stomach and buried his face in his arms. If there was crying to be done, it had better be done silently. But despite all he could do, he allowed a sob to escape aloud. And then he felt a rag being shoved roughly into one hand.

"Here, use this!" It was Beetle's voice coming through the darkness. The sound of his voice was immediately followed by the sound of a match being struck.

Taddy rolled his head over and saw a stub of lighted candle in Beetle's hand, with Beetle's face peering over it.

"Your nose is still droozling," said Beetle. "Wipe it."

Taddy did, while looking sideways at Beetle. Now he was really going to be in for it. As if he did not have enough to be miserable about, Beetle had caught him crying. But Beetle had begun to rummage around in the corner behind his head. Out came what looked like another wadded-up rag. Beetle unfolded it and shoved it toward Taddy.

"It's just a bit of muffing I saved for you," said Beetle.

"There's some more stuff too, bits of meat and vedge and the like, all kindness of Mrs. Scrat."

Taddy looked into the rag. Yes, what Beetle had said was there was indeed there. And jumbled all together though it was, the smell was a torment to his empty stomach. But he just stared at the food without touching anything. For was it not a bit of muffin that had plunged him into so much trouble already?

"Look here," said Beetle, "I know wot's on your mind. The picter of wot happened to you last time you took a bite of muffing is running through your head. I know you ain't got much reason to trust me, but if you cornsider it, you ain't got much reason not to. Think on it."

Taddy still hesitated. Why would Beetle take the risk of saving food for him? Was this a trap or a trick arranged by Neezer to test him?

"Eat it!" said Beetle.

And then suddenly, Taddy no longer cared if it was a trap. He did not care that Beetle was staring at him searchingly over the flickering candle. He did not care about anything but getting that food inside him. He grabbed a handful and shoved it into his mouth. Then another handful. And another. He never stopped until the last crumb and greasy morsel was scraped from the sodden rag, and every last bit of flavor licked from his fingers. And it was only then that he stopped to think of what he had done. He looked fearfully into the dark kitchen.

Beetle scowled. "Look, Toady, I much as told you you got nuffing to be scared about. *Nuffing,* you hear me? Leastways not regarding this grand meal you just put away. Neezer knows nuffing about it, nor what Mrs. Scrat put in. I promise you. And somefing about me you will find out, if you ain't already, is I am a man of my word."

"But . . . but why did you do it?" asked Taddy, still suspicious. After all, it was almost impossible to accept that the Beetle now beside him was not exactly the same Beetle of a few hours earlier.

"Maybe 'cause you been getting it a lot rougher'n I did when I first got interdooced to the Dog's Tail." Beetle shrugged uncomfortably, as if embarrassed at having to reveal there was a heart beating somewhere inside his skinny little chest. "That mean dog in the picter only knows *I* got it rough enough."

"But you could have been caught," said Taddy.

"Could have," replied Beetle. "Wasn't though. Anyway, I would have just lied. Told him it was for me."

"I . . . I thought you said you were a man of your word," said Taddy.

"Don't be a raving ninny," replied Beetle, sounding more like his former self of several hours earlier. "In my line of business, which is taking care of my skin, I ain't one to use the same rules wiv the likes of Neezer. I places a high walue on my life, and acts accordingly."

"Well, thank you all the same, Beetle," said Taddy. "I'm sorry I forgot to say it."

"No bovver," said Beetle. "But while you're at it, you might just as well say 'thank you' for me getting you out of the icehouse quick as any wink."

Taddy's fifteen minutes in the icehouse hardly felt like a quick wink, but if Beetle, the expert on such things, said it was so, then it must be so.

"How did you do that?" Taddy asked.

"Reminded Neezer as how a puny subjec' like you no doubt wouldn't last out five minutes in that igloo. But as puny as you might be, I told him, you're still good for somefing, and costing no more'n a few scraps from the top of the table, and a bed under it. Those items might be more waluable than I had allowed, I likewise told him, but my cornsideration was that he ought to think about it."

"What . . . what did Neezer say to that?" asked Taddy, enormously impressed.

Beetle grimaced. "Oh, he snarled and snapped as is usual for Neezer, noting as how I was risen above my station and needed a lesson. I believe I almost got myself throwed in the icehouse alongside of you, I do. Anyways, he cornsulted with Lucky as usual, and did as usual wot he was going to anyway. Which was, in this case, not to throw me in and to let you out."

"Thank you for that as well," said Taddy. "I doubt I could have lasted much longer."

"No bovver again," replied Beetle.

"But you know something," said Taddy. "I think you didn't get put in the icehouse because . . . because they like you now."

"Like me? Ha!" snorted Beetle. "Your brain's turned to mush, Toady. All they like's my free muscles. Lose them, and back I get sent to the bottom of the line. I got a big picter in my mind about just how much Neezer and Lucky's in love wiv me."

"Beetle," said Taddy, "what . . . what *do* they have on you?"

Beetle's head jerked up, and he looked sharply at Taddy. Then he returned to staring over the candle, a far-away look in his eyes as if he had not heard the question. At last, he sighed and gave a shrug.

"I guess you got a right to know, seeing as how I know wot I know about you. So this is how it is. You see, Pa was a sailor once. He met Ma in London and brought her to New York, which makes you and me bofe from the same location, as it turns up. Anyways, Pa used to beat me twice a day when he was in port, wevver I needed it or not. When he stopped being a sailor and worked on the docks, I got beat a whole lot more'n I cornsidered I needed. Ma couldn't stop him, though she tried. Then Ma died, and nobody was left to try. So I corncluded I'd get back to London to Ma's folks, if she had any, and if I could find them. You paying attention, Toady? You ain't falling asleep or anyfing?"

Taddy shook his head. There was no way that he would fall asleep now!

"Well then," Beetle continued, "I stowed away on a ship wot I thought was bound for London, only it turned out to be a ship bound for here. When I was wandering around thinking over how to find anovver ship going in the right direction, I bumped into Neezer on the docks. I reported my story, hoping as how he could help me. So he helped me into the Dog's Tail, and told me I'd be heading back to Pa if I tried to run off. Which makes me a bigger ninny'n you ever thought of being. So you can see as how I got myself just as stuck here as you. And what I think is you and me had best hang together, or we will drown separate. Shake on that?"

Taddy did not need a second invitation. He reached over at once, and the two boys solemnly shook hands.

"Now," said Beetle, yawning hugely, "cornsidering what hour it is and what hour it's soon going to be, we'd better get to sleep." He abruptly blew out the candle and dropped his head on his arms. "G'night!"

Taddy was taken aback at this sudden end to their conversation. He had the feeling that something in it was still missing. Could it be the word *friends*? Beetle had now handed Taddy a "big stick" over him by making his confession. But were you friends just because you each held a stick over the head of the other? They had shaken hands, but was that not more to seal a business bargain than a friendship?

Yet on the other hand, what about Beetle risking punishment to bring Taddy food and have him rescued from the icehouse? Well, what *about* that?

"Beetle?"

"Wot now? You ain't droozling again?"

"No, I just wanted to know why you brought me food, and then got me rescued from the icehouse."

"I already told you."

"Was that really and truly the reason?"

"Course it wasn't really and truly the reason, ninny." This was said crossly. "That reason was just what jumped into my mind. The rock-bottom trufe is I didn't want you starved to deaf or froze to deaf, 'cause then it's back to me doing all the work. *Now* you satisfied?"

Taddy's heart tightened into a cold, hard knot. So that was the reason! He should have known better than to think being friends had anything to do with all of this.

Beetle was right about one thing—he was indeed a prize ninny! Well, he was certainly not going to droozle again and have Beetle think that he cared so much as one penny's worth.

Minutes went by. And then from the dark came Beetle's voice sleepily. "Maybe I just did it because everyone's got to have a friend in this world, Toady . . . even me."

Chapter VIII
A Satisfactory Explanation

The next morning, Taddy was awakened by something being jerked out roughly from under his shoulder.

"My droozle rag," muttered Beetle. "Got to save that."

Through half-open eyes, Taddy saw Beetle carefully hanging up the rag on a nail behind him as if it were some great treasure. Beside it hung another rag, somewhat filthier, as it was the one wrapped around the food served to Taddy earlier.

"You finally got your peepers open," said Beetle, sounding almost angry. "'Bout time. Mrs. Scrat's here, and the rules ain't changed since yesterday, near as I can tell." That message delivered, he scurried out from under the table as fast as any insect that ever bore his name. It was as if he were trying to escape from Taddy.

Mrs. Scrat was already at work scooping flour into a large enamel basin. "Beetle," she said, "you had best share the wood chore evenly with Toady, or you'll be late again in the tavern. Then we'll *all* hear about it."

Beetle just shrugged and then disappeared out the back door. Taddy was close on his heels, but hesitated at the door and turned back. "M-M-Mrs. Scrat . . ." he began.

Mrs. Scrat raised her eyes from her work for a moment, then quickly dropped them again. But it was enough for Taddy to have seen the fear in them. "It's all right, Toady. I know," she said. "Run along now."

It was certain that the subject of food smuggled under the table was not to be brought up, or given thanks for. There could be nothing more said about it.

It also appeared certain, at least for the morning, that nothing much was to be said about anything by anyone, especially Beetle. If he wanted Taddy for a friend, he had an odd way of showing it. Sunk in his own thoughts, he hardly spoke to Taddy as they delivered the loads of wood. Every effort Taddy made at conversation was met only by a muttered reply. Or no reply at all.

In the tavern, as they scuttled about setting tables and serving food, there was hardly an opportunity for talking. But Beetle was downright surly, especially when they were near Neezer and Lucky.

"Watch out where you're going, clumsy!" he said in a voice loud enough to be picked up by the two men.

Then, under their very noses, Beetle suddenly gave Taddy a sharp jab in the ribs, so the top plate of a stack he was carrying went sailing out and crashing to the floor.

For a moment, this seemed to startle even Beetle. But he quickly recovered himself. "Now you've done it, stoopid!" he said fiercely, throwing a look at Neezer and Lucky to make certain they had not missed the point. They had not.

"You'll pay for that!" Neezer snarled under his breath. "There's no time for another little lesson in the icehouse, but see he gets nothing to eat this morning, Lucky. That'll teach him to be more careful of my china."

An escape from the icehouse, but nothing to eat until the crusts shared with Lucky at their noonday "picnic" on the ice wagon! It seemed to Taddy that he was spared being frozen to death only to be starved to death instead.

As he scraped up the bits of shattered china from the floor, he was torn between misery and burning rage at Beetle. What kind of cat-and-mouse game was he playing, making Taddy think they were friends, only to turn on him when it suited him to do so? Was this Beetle's idea of being a friend? Better to have an enemy than such a friend as this! And come to think of it, was anything that Beetle had told him really true? If not, then Taddy once again had nothing at all on Beetle, while Beetle still had a great deal on *him*. But not everything!

For Beetle still did not know about the danger Taddy was in outside the Dog's Tail, or about his twin. Good thing Beetle had so suddenly blown out the candle and gone off to sleep. For Taddy had been on the point of revealing his whole story!

Well, never mind Beetle. Taddy knew he had something more important to think about as he sat shivering on the ice wagon beside Lucky—Jeremy. What should Taddy do when he saw his twin again? What was he to say? Should he try to hide his face and not risk having someone discover how much they looked alike? As it turned out, however, there was no need to answer those questions.

When they arrived at the Mainyard house, Mrs. Mainyard was summoned to the kitchen as was expected. But instead of a trip to the icehouse, she called Lucky aside and held a low-voiced conversation with him, all the while glancing over at Taddy. Had she noticed how much he and Jeremy looked alike? What would be done about it? What was she revealing to Lucky? How much more danger would Taddy now be in? But Taddy was not to know the result of that conversation, at least not then. When he and Lucky left the Mainyard house, nothing was said about it. And Jeremy had never appeared in the kitchen. Not once!

Then, on the way back to the Dog's Tail, something happened that for a few joyful moments drove all thoughts of either Beetle or Jeremy from his mind.

"Rats!" Lucky muttered as they approached Diggles's Bakery in the wagon. "Forgot Mrs. Diggles told me to come back today. Rats! I'll have to stop."

Stop they did, with Lucky grumbling about his aching legs all the way to the door. They met the cheerful Mrs. Diggles in her kitchen with at least three children clustered about her skirts. To Lucky's clear disappointment, she did indeed want her order of ice that day. It was after the ice had been delivered, and he was trailing Lucky on their way out, that Taddy felt a tug on his jacket. He looked around quickly, thinking it was done by one of the children. Instead, there stood Mrs. Diggles herself. With twinkling eyes, she thrust a small package into his jacket pocket.

"They're cinnamon raisin," she whispered. Then she smiled and put a finger to her lips.

Taddy was so startled, he stood rooted to the spot. Mrs. Diggles gave him a little push forward. "Hurry! Hurry!" she breathed, and Taddy darted after Lucky.

A cinnamon raisin cookie! Could there be as many as

two? Cinnamon cookies no doubt from that tantalizing heap on Mrs. Diggles's kitchen table! Taddy could smell the cinnamon wafting from his pocket as the wagon rumbled down the streets to the Dog's Tail. Was it possible that Lucky could do so as well? But that individual just sat hunched up on his seat, grousing under his breath about his aching legs, and clearly smelling nothing. Not a delicious cinnamon fragrance coming from his seatmate, at any rate!

Taddy did not dare take the package out even to look at it when they arrived. He just shoved his jacket under the table as always. But the package never left his mind, not for a moment. He thought about it as he was scurrying around setting the tables in the tavern. He thought about it while he was carrying out the dirty platters and dishes. He even thought about it while he was snatching scraps off the dishes. Especially then! Oh, how he looked forward to the moment when he would bite into that tender, fragrant, flavorful cinnamon raisin delight! And oh, the joy of knowing that nobody else had had a bite of it first!

He would have it that night, he decided, after Beetle had gone to sleep. That could be very late, but never mind. He would just stay awake, waiting. All he had left to decide was whether he should have the treat all at once, or make it last for another night. Well, at least he did not have to share it with Beetle. It was to be for Taddy alone. Too bad for Beetle. Serve him right!

Once again the kitchen was hushed and dark, and Taddy lay under the table wide awake. But he was not tossing and turning as he had been the night before. He lay silent and still, staring at the table top over him, hardly daring to blink for fear of making a sound. It was Beetle instead who tossed and turned this night. What was taking him so long to fall asleep? Taddy could hardly bear the thought that he himself would fall asleep first. Thump! Thump! Over went Beetle again. Thump! Thump! Thump!

What was troubling Beetle that was making it so difficult for him to fall asleep? His life seemed almost soft and comfortable now compared to Taddy's. Or was it? He certainly worked just as hard as Taddy around the tavern. He had no more to eat or more comfortable quarters. And who was to know how easy it was to be under Neezer's thumb the rest of the day? But most important of all, was Beetle not just as much a prisoner of the Dog's Tail as Taddy himself?

For somehow, deep inside, Taddy felt that Beetle's story had been true. It was impossible to believe, hard as Taddy tried, that he had invented the tale he told. No, Taddy was certain that they were both in the same grim boat. And it was just as certain that, for *whatever* reason, Beetle had come to his rescue the night before. There could be no argument about *that*.

"Beetle?" he said softly.

A few moments of silence passed. "Wot?"

"Would . . . would you please light the candle again?"

There was another longer silence. Then came the wary reply. "Wot for?"

"It's a surprise," said Taddy.

"I don't like surprises," was the ungracious reply.

"You'll like this one," said Taddy.

The silence following this was so long that Taddy

thought Beetle must have finally dropped off to sleep. Then he heard the sound of a match being lit. The candle in Beetle's hand flared up, with Beetle's suspicious face peering over it.

"Well, wot's this surprise?"

Taddy quickly plunged a hand into his jacket pocket and drew out the package hidden there by Mrs. Diggles. He still had no idea how many cookies were wrapped up in the brown paper. For all he knew, there was only one.

Slowly, carefully, he unwrapped the paper. And there they lay—*three* large, fragrant, raisin-laden, cinnamon cookies. *Three* of them! Three that might all have been for Taddy. Instead, he studiedly broke one of them into two equal pieces. Then he picked up a whole cookie and held it out with the half cookie to Beetle.

Wooden-faced, Beetle stared at the cookies without touching them. "Where'd they come from?"

"Mrs. Diggles gave them to me," replied Taddy.

"Lucky let you have 'em?" said Beetle.

"He didn't know about it," Taddy said. "Mrs. Diggles stuffed them into my pocket secretly when we were leaving. Lucky never saw her. Go on, take them. They're yours."

"Did Mrs. Diggles say so?" asked Beetle.

"No," said Taddy. "But that doesn't matter. They're from me. Now, will you please take them?"

Beetle finally gave in, but he acted as if he thought the cookies would snap back at him as he took them from Taddy's hand. "Wot did you want for them?" he asked.

"Nothing," said Taddy. "Why would I want any-thing?"

"Because nobody gives away somefing for nuffing, that's why," Beetle muttered.

"*You* did," said Taddy. "You brought me some food and had me rescued from the icehouse. You did that for nothing"—Taddy hesitated—"didn't you?"

Beetle thought this over for a moment and then gave a thoroughly honest grin. "Well, so I did. And I never asked anyfing for it, did I?"

"No, you didn't," said Taddy, and meant it.

But Beetle's grin suddenly vanished. "Still don't know why you should be giving me anyfing." He looked at Taddy warily. "Ain't you noticed how I been behaving?"

"Yes," replied Taddy, for what was the use of lying?

"And I suppose you likewise noted wot happened in the tavern under Neezer's and Lucky's noses?" Beetle carefully avoided Taddy's steady gaze.

"I . . . I did," replied Taddy.

"And it didn't make you angry?" asked Beetle.

"It . . . it did," replied Taddy.

Beetle shifted uncomfortably. "And you still wish me to have these cookies?"

"I . . . I do," said Taddy. "It's for practically saving my life, Beetle."

"Oh, that was nuffing," said Beetle. "I'd do that again, I would. But it was our conwersation afterward wot I got to worrying over, rewealing everyfing 'bout my ma and pa, and how Neezer tricked me, and the whole lot. Well, when you cornsider it, I didn't need to say anyfing, now did I? I thought as how I was the biggest ninny that ever was. I wished I could take it all back."

"Do you still wish that?" asked Taddy.

"I ain't certain," said Beetle. "But I'll tell you somefing else. Wot I did in the tavern had nuffing to do wiv that. I just decided that if Neezer and Lucky cornsider for one minute that you and me got anyfing to do wiv one another beside being fellow slaveys of the Dog's Tail, well . . ." Beetle drew a finger across his throat. "Maybe I should have told you wot I was going to do before I did it. But I never meant for you to drop the plate. I never meant to hit you so hard."

"It's all right, Beetle," said Taddy. "At least I didn't get thrown into the icehouse!"

"No, you didn't," agreed Beetle. "But do we have to look at the cookies all night? Ain't we going to eat them now?"

"It's what they're for," replied Taddy.

"Well, should we eat them slow or quick?" asked Beetle.

"Slow," said Taddy. "We'll make them last as long as we can."

The boys started nibbling at the cookies, each trying to outdo the other in slowness. But they ended up nibbling faster and faster, finally stuffing down the last bite. Then they licked and licked their fingers until every last bit of cinnamon flavor had long since disappeared.

When Beetle finally blew out the candle and they dropped down onto their hard beds, there was no more thumping and thumping on the part of anyone unable to go to sleep. And there was no way of telling who drifted off sooner. All Taddy knew was that when he next opened his eyes, it was not to the light of a candle, but to the gray light of morning making its way under the table where they both had slept.

Chapter IX
Rub, Rub, Rub

Taddy's heart was now as light as it had been before he lost his aunt and uncle Buntz and all the terrible events that followed thereafter. For now he really believed he had found a friend, even though one in the unlikely form of Beetle. But Beetle was right; the friendship must be kept a secret. Neezer and Lucky must never know that they were more than "fellow slaveys of the Dog's Tail."

But Taddy did not mind. He did not even mind when Beetle grumped at him about some imagined clumsiness in the tavern in front of the ever watchful Neezer and Lucky. For was that grump not accompanied right on its heels by a secret raising of Beetle's eyebrow and a big wink? Taddy had to bite his lip to keep from grinning!

Then one morning, nearly a week after he and Beetle had sealed their friendship with Mrs. Diggles's cookies in the dead of night, Taddy was passing in front of Neezer in the tavern, when a long arm reached out and grabbed him by the collar. Taddy's heart jumped into his throat. All he could think was that he and Beetle had been found out after all!

"Not so fast, boy," Neezer growled. "We got something to say to you." He studied Taddy up and down with calculating eyes. "I don't know how much help *you'll* be," he concluded finally, "but Mrs. Main'ard delivered me a message care of Lucky last week, and it appears as how she wishes your services as cook's and maid's helper . . . pantry boy, she calls it. So, as your services here can be done without, and no great loss, you're to be working for the Widow Main'ard, starting today. Maybe there you'll be worth something after all. I'll see she pays well for her new *pantry* boy."

"Am . . . am I to be *paid*?" Taddy stammered.

"*You* be paid? That's a rare one, ain't it, Lucky? No, it's *me* who's to be paid, you little weasel. And you see to it you do the best job you ever done in your skinny little life, or I'll know the reason why."

"What-what about talking?" asked Taddy.

"What's *what* about talking. Talking's talking. You being smart with me, boy?" Neezer gave Taddy's shoulder a sharp shake.

"L-L-Lucky said I wasn't to talk to anyone when we delivered ice," said Taddy, faltering. "I mean, excepting him."

"Don't be stoopid," Lucky butted in, with a quick look at Neezer to make certain he himself was not the one in that category. "Naterally you got to talk to someone else when I ain't there. You just ain't allowed to *say* anything, anything what matters. Ain't that right, Neezer?"

"You got it exactly right," said Neezer. "Anyways, 'yes, ma'am' and 'no, ma'am' is all that ought to be coming out of you. And then do as you're told. Anything else, and I'll hear about it. You can count on it! Is that clear?"

Yes, it was clear, and also clearly amazing. Going to work for Mrs. Mainyard at the grand big house! So *that* had been the subject of her private conversation with Lucky. Although the SCRAT'S ICE AND ODD JOBS wagon had returned to the Mainyard house since that time, it was only to deliver ice for the icebox in the kitchen, and no one had been present but Mrs. Fry. Taddy had finally decided that the private conversation must have had nothing to do with how much Jeremy and he looked alike, and he had all but forgotten about it. Now he knew that he, at least, had been a subject of the conversation after all, but who could have guessed that it was in such a surprising way? Still, could anything good come from any arrangement made by Neezer and Lucky? What did Beetle think about it? Taddy soon found out.

"Well, you fell into it, you did," Beetle whispered out of the corner of his mouth. "Working for Mrs. Mainyard. Wot a cushy job! Wish I'd got it."

With Beetle's seal of approval, there was surely nothing for Taddy to worry about. Except Jeremy! Now they would be working together. If nobody knew it now, they would soon see how much the boys looked like one another. And what was to come of *that*? What, indeed!

"Now, Toady, as you've been told, Miss Madelina and Miss Dora are both down with the influenza. Their teacher has been notified, so he won't be coming today, which mercifully means no special trays to be prepared. But Mary and I will still be extra busy today. So you're to be very careful *downstairs,* which is where you're to be working."

This information, and accompanying warning, were

delivered to Taddy by a stern, unsmiling Mrs. Fry, who turned out to be housekeeper as well as cook. Beside her stood Mary, the housemaid, full of lofty, fifteen-year-old importance at being along with Mrs. Fry as she instructed Taddy in his new Mainyard household duties.

"First thing you do," continued Mrs. Fry, "is bring all that silver from the dining table and sideboard to the kitchen. *Very* carefully, and no more than two pieces at a time, mind you. Later you'll be polishing all of it before it goes back, carried in the same way, I might remind you. After that, you will dust everything in this room, including the baseboards, which I can promise you will be noted by Mrs. Mainyard, whatever *you'd* like to think about it. Then you're to put a bit of the lemon oil on a rag from your bucket and rub, rub, rub the table and sideboard. And mind you, there's to be no dawdling. Now, come along, Mary!"

Wiping her hands on her apron as if to say she had done her job and could now wipe Taddy out of her mind, Mrs. Fry bustled out, with the self-important Mary bobbing along behind her.

For a few moments, Taddy stood perfectly still in the high-ceilinged, cavernous dining room. Only his eyes moved, wandering across the long, gleaming mahogany dining table (could its glowing top possibly be improved upon by rub, rub, rubbing it with an oil rag?) to the sideboard spread with an enormous silver tea service and three silver platters of richest silver design. A dozen carved mahogany dining chairs with red velvet seats trimmed in gold braid stood stiffly at attention like so many soldiers put there to guard all this magnificence.

Well, they didn't have to worry about Taddy. For he

intended to rub, rub, rub whether something needed it or not, and to scrub, scrub, scrub, and dust, dust, dust in the same manner. For this job was a world away from riding around all day with Lucky, or working in the tavern of the Dog's Tail.

Why, almost as soon as he had entered the kitchen and Lucky had left (not forgetting, naturally, to issue the usual warnings), Taddy had been served by Mrs. Fry with a bowl of steaming oatmeal with sugar and cream, and even bread and butter to go along with it. He had then been sent into a small bathroom, miraculously right off the kitchen, there to wash up and change into the suit of clothes he was to wear until he had to return to the Dog's Tail that evening. So now he stood with a filled stomach, dressed in a clean flannel shirt and trousers exactly like the ones Jeremy had worn, which fitted him amazingly well.

But where *was* Jeremy? Was he at work someplace else in this vast house? When was Taddy ever to see him? At the moment it was difficult to imagine that there was anyone at all but himself in the house. Once Mrs. Fry's and Mary's footsteps had faded, everything had fallen silent. Thick carpets and rich velvet drapes muffled any sounds that might have ventured in from the street. Within the hushed dining room, only an occasional timid gurgle from the radiator broke the silence.

But Taddy knew he could not continue standing there, letting his thoughts wander. Quickly he crept to the sideboard where the magnificent silver tea service glistened on a tray wreathed in a garland of silver grapes and ivy leaves. Biting his lower lip and holding his breath, Taddy gently lifted up the teapot.

"Good morning, Toady!"

At the sound of the voice, Taddy let go the tea pot, and it fell onto the tray with a sickening clatter. He whirled around to see Mrs. Mainyard standing in the doorway to the dining room. Had she been standing there all along, watching him? Did she think he was *dawdling,* as Mrs. Fry had put it? Worse, would she think him so clumsy she would send him back in disgrace to the Dog's Tail? Taddy's heart was in his throat as he stared, frozen, at his beautiful new mistress.

But Mrs. Mainyard was smiling. "I'm afraid I startled you," she said. "Don't be frightened. I'm sure no damage was done. Next time you'll be more careful, won't you?"

His eyes riveted on Mrs. Mainyard, Taddy nodded.

"I'm certain of it," she said. "You appear to be a good, honest boy, and I think I did not make a mistake in having you here. But, of course, you must prove that to me. Now, I must not keep you from your work, so please go right along with what Mrs. Fry has asked you to do."

Mrs. Mainyard rewarded the transfixed Taddy with another smile. Then, with her rose silk skirts rustling softly around her ankles, she stepped lightly over to a window, where she stood delicately adjusting a fold in the velvet drapery.

Once again, Taddy lifted up the silver teapot, holding it so tightly his fingertips were white. As he carried it to the doorway, he looked quickly over his shoulder at Mrs. Mainyard. Was she watching to see how very careful he was being? But Mrs. Mainyard was deeply intent on the drapery. Taddy did not know whether she was even aware that he was still in the room.

One thing he was certain of, however. He was not going to do a good job just for the privilege of being well fed, or having warm, clean clothes, or being able to work in this rich, elegant house. No, he would do a good job to please Mrs. Mainyard. He would prove to her that she had made no mistake when she invited him into her home!

Furthermore, he knew that whatever happened with him or with Jeremy, there would never ever be any danger for either of them in this house. Not as long as Mrs. Mainyard lived in it!

Chapter X

A Trip to the Cellar

"Well, go on, go on, Toady!" Mrs. Fry exclaimed impatiently. "Nothing down there's going to bite you. Oh, I never did see such a day! With the girls and their influenza, half the upstairs work unfinished, and me having to train *you* into the bargain, what's to be next? Thank fortune it's six o'clock, and the day almost ended. Now, don't forget to wipe your feet on the mat before you put one toe back in here. All we need is for you to go traipsing coal dust all over the house!" Mrs. Fry rushed out of the kitchen, throwing up her hands as she repeated in a despairing voice, "That's *all* we need!"

Taddy, of course, had been unfortunate enough to hesitate on the landing of the door to the cellar. Now, clutching the damp brick walls on either side, he started down the steep, narrow stairway. Slowly, one careful foot after the other, down, down, down he crept. Certain that each step would send him plunging all the way, he finally reached the cellar floor.

And felt as if he had stepped into another world! For how different from the warm, velvet-draped richness of the house overhead was this dark, dank, dismal corridor lit only by tiny gaslights that peered out from the walls like pale, flickering eyes. They weakly lit up another dark stairwell leading to the street, the open door at the far end that Mrs. Fry had told him was the coal room, and at least seven closed doors indicating the presence of other rooms crouching in the shadows. Taddy threw his arms around himself and shivered as, half running, half stumbling on the clammy brick floor, he started down the corridor. Then suddenly he saw something that brought him to a sharp stop.

It was a small, cracked oval mirror hanging on the wall directly across from a gaslight. The tiny reflection of the light broke into bits as it fluttered over the crack, and it was this that had caught the corner of Taddy's eye as he ran past. But there was something there of far greater interest than the mirror. For under it was a narrow wooden shelf. And on the shelf was an array of objects whose shapes were of heart-stopping delight to Taddy. He inched cautiously toward it.

What he looked at on the shelf, laid neatly in a row, were a top, a small rubber ball followed by a space where something might once have been, then a little sack that looked as if it held marbles, a frayed piece of rope that could have served as a skip rope, a small mound of pebbles, a dented penknife, a pencil stub, and three bent nails—all things that could be dear to a young boy. Jeremy! These must be Jeremy's things—his treasured possessions. Could this be the place where Jeremy sometimes stole away to play?

Taddy reached out his hand to touch the little sack. It

was of soft, worn leather, drawn tightly together at the top with a bit of string. And yes, he could tell, it did hold marbles. These were marbles Jeremy must have rolled on the rough brick floor, the ball he had bounced, and the rope he had skipped with.

Slowly, Taddy raised his eyes and looked into the cracked mirror, so much like the one he had once had. The face he saw, its reflection cut in two by the crack, must have looked back countless times on a face just like it—Jeremy's face. Why, it almost seemed that if you replaced a half of one boy's reflection with that of the other, it would match the remaining one exactly! Suddenly, tears stung Taddy's eyes. His own brother! His twin!

But where was he? It was now six o'clock, and Taddy had yet to see him. Where was Jeremy? *Where?* And then Taddy had a startling thought. What if Jeremy *lived* in this cellar instead of returning someplace else each night, as Taddy himself would be doing? What if he were there right now behind one of those closed doors? Was there time to look? Taddy felt his heart begin to thump hard. Then he took a deep breath and started out.

He crept up to the first door and, with a hesitant hand, tapped on it lightly. There was no answer. He tapped again. The tap was greeted by silence. He reached out a hand and slowly turned the handle. The hinges squeaked a little, but the door opened easily. One inch. Two inches. Then all the way. Cautiously, Taddy peered in.

Light from the corridor, dim though it was, was just enough to reveal that this was nothing more than a dusty storeroom piled with boxes, barrels, and an odd table and chair. It was certainly not a room where anyone would be living. Taddy closed the door softly and ran swiftly on tip-toes to the next one.

This room proved to be much larger, and held great copper tubs, crimped washboards hanging on the walls, two ironing boards, and several irons lined up for heating on a coal stove. It was evident that this was the laundry room. And the next one also left no doubt as to its purpose, for great hams hung on hooks from its ceiling; flour and molasses barrels loomed in the corners; and its shelves were stacked with tins and jars and boxes of tea and sugar, pickles and preserves, spices and biscuits, and every other imaginable kind of food.

Now there were three doors left to try. One proved to be only another storage room. The second was no more rewarding than the first. There was now only one room left, but by now Taddy had decided that his idea of Jeremy living in the cellar was more wishful thinking than anything. Expecting to find only another storage room, Taddy boldly reached out for the door handle. And the handle began to turn on its own!

The hinges of the door groaned. The door opened slowly. Shuffle, thud. Shuffle, thud. Someone came limping through the doorway, one foot dragging behind the other. The room behind him was dimly visible, courtesy of a quivering gaslight on the wall and an oil lamp on a table. It was a sparsely furnished room lived in by some-one, but if this was the person, then the someone was clearly not Jeremy.

It was instead a grizzled old man, with hair more white than otherwise. A pipe-stem neck attached a large head to his short, hunched body. The head, poking through the opening of an oversized jersey, gave the impression of a goblin emerging from a hole. Refining this impression was the fact that he wore a pair of enormous, shabby leather slippers, much too large for his feet. It was these, plus a crippled leg, that caused him to shuffle and thud as he walked. Shuffle, thud. Shuffle, thud. He drew near the rigid Taddy, peering at him with squinted eyes. A crooked grin suddenly creased the old man's wizened face, remaining only long enough to display gums with some three missing teeth, before just as suddenly disappearing.

"Dum de dum dum, dum, dum, dum," he sang tunelessly, studying Taddy's face. "Thought so! Thought my ears caught something—or more likely some*one*—prowling about. What I don't see, my ears always makes up for. Dum de dum dum. Now, pull *your* eyes back into your head, little man, or they'll pop right onto the bricks and bust into smithereens. Dum de dum dum, dum, dum, dum." The old man gave another short-lived grin. Then he scowled. "Where'd you come from?"

Warned so many times not to say anything "what matters," or for that matter, much of anything at all, Taddy was by now thoroughly tongue-tied. And how was the old man's question to be answered with a "yes, sir," or "no, sir"? All Taddy was able to do was stare back at him.

The old man raised an eyebrow. "Dum de dum dum. Well, let's try another one, and see if the cat'll let go your tongue. You got a name?"

Too frightened to answer, too frightened *not* to, Taddy finally stammered, "It's . . . it's T-T-Toady."

"Toady, Toady, Toady," sang the old man. "Dum de dum dum. Another little man sent down for coal. And got yourself lost finding the furnace room, I'll wager. I know it well, Toady. No one knows better. Chieftain of the furnace room. Keeper of the cellar. That's old Simon!"

Shuffle, thud. Shuffle, thud. His slippers flapping on the bricks, he started off down the corridor, singing under his breath. "Dum de dum dum, dum, dum, dum. Simple Simon met a pieman going to the fair; says Simple Simon to the pieman, ''Ware, beware, beware.' Dum de dum dum. Dum de dum dum. Simple Simon met a pieman. Dum de dum dum."

When they came to the cracked mirror with the shelf under it, the old man hesitated and stopped. His large head swiveled around on its pipe-stem neck so he could peer into the mirror. Then his head swiveled back, and he squinted his eyes at Taddy. What was he thinking about? Was it possible that he was comparing Taddy with Jeremy? Had he with his half-blind eyes discovered how much they looked alike? If so, what use would he make of the information?

But if the old man had made any discoveries, there were none he wished to talk about. Shuffle, thud. Shuffle, thud. He was on his way to the furnace room again with no apparent interest in trying to have any further conversations with Taddy.

"Dum de dum dum." Content with listening to the sound of his own voice singing his tuneless little song, he stayed glued to Taddy until he had collected his bucket of coal and was on his way back up the stairs.

"Dum de dum dum, dum, dum, dum."

Taddy could hear the voice trailing after him all the way as he struggled up the stairs. He could not escape fast enough from the gloomy cellar, and from this strange and frightening old man.

How grateful Taddy was that this was to be his only trip to the cellar that day. If only it could be his only trip there forever! But every evening at the stroke of six, just before Lucky came to pick him up in the wagon, it was to be Taddy's duty to fetch a bucket of coal for the drawing room fireplace. And there was no reason to think he would ever be relieved of this miserable ending to his workdays at the Mainyard house.

Chapter XI

The Gentleman in Black

The tolling of the tall, ponderous grandfather clock shattered the silence of the entrance in the Mainyard house.

Bong! Bong! Bong! Bong!

Taddy very nearly dropped the eggshell-thin cups and saucers he was cautiously transporting from the dining room to the kitchen. They shook in his hands with the small, clickety-click sound of teeth chattering in a cold wind. Taddy wondered if he would ever get used to these sudden, loud announcements of the time as he passed through the hall.

The faint sounds of girls' voices drifted down the stairwell from the upper reaches of the house. They belonged to Madelina and Dora, yet to be seen again by Taddy because they had been confined upstairs with their influenza the whole while he had been there. They must be back in their schoolroom attending to their studies, Taddy thought. For earlier that day, before Mary (to Mrs. Fry's dismay) had suddenly come down with Miss

Madelina's and Miss Dora's complaint and been sent home, she had answered the doorbell and reported that it was the girls' teacher returning. But beyond the occasional hum of sounds from upstairs, the house, muffled in its thick carpets and heavy draperies, was hushed as always.

The tolling of the grandfather clock had no sooner stopped echoing in the entrance hall than the jarring ring of the doorbell shattered the silence again. And it was Taddy who would have to answer it in Mary's absence. Cups and saucers rattling dangerously in his hands, he scurried to the kitchen. Then he flew back to the front door, reciting to himself all Mrs. Fry's instructions. Breathless when he arrived, he swallowed a big gulp of air and opened one of the heavy oak doors. And promptly forgot everything Mrs. Fry had told him.

For Taddy found himself facing a man so cold and motionless he might well have been a statue carved of granite. Black granite. Because he was dressed all in black, from his polished black shoes to his elegantly tapered trousers, to his stylishly fitted overcoat of finest black wool and onyx buttons, to his black leather gloves, one of which was curled around an ebony walking stick. The handle of the latter was his only concession to a color other than black, for it was a fox's head fashioned of pure gleaming gold.

But it was something else that caused Taddy to stand before him, paralyzed. For above a brief black beard, perfectly clipped, and a pale aristocratic nose was a pair of chilling, calculating eyes that went through Taddy as if they had been made of cold steel. The eyes studied Taddy through half-closed eyelids for one, two, three, four, five freezing seconds. But if they discovered anything, there was no way of telling, for the man's face never changed its frigid expression.

"Well," he snapped finally, "will you be standing there all day? Or will you have the kindness to stand aside and let me in?"

"Y-y-yes, s-s-sir," stammered Toady, opening the door wider and stepping back into the hall.

The man then, with great deliberation, leaned over to pick up two identical white boxes tied together with gold cord that sat on the porch at his feet. After this, he finally stepped into the house.

By now, Taddy had managed to remember one of Mrs. Fry's instructions. "M-m-may I take your coat, sir?"

The man nodded curtly. "But first," he said, "I wish you to take these boxes and set them on that chair over there. And be careful, please. The contents are fragile."

Now, whether what happened next was actually intended by the man, or whether it was a true accident, Taddy did not know. He was almost certain, however, that when he reached for the boxes, the man let go of them before Taddy had a grip on them. They fell to the floor with a terrible thud.

The man's face twisted with rage. "You clumsy idiot!" he said furiously. Then he grabbed Taddy by the collar with such force that he nearly tore the shirt from Taddy's shoulder. "I told you to be careful! It's a good thing those boxes fell on the carpet and their contents were well wrapped, for if anything happened to them . . ." He let go of Taddy, snatched up the boxes, and strode with them to the chair. Then he peeled off his gloves angrily and jammed them into his pocket. Finally, he removed his coat.

"Now, let's see if you can manage *this* any better," he said. But he hesitated a moment, still holding the coat. "By the way, what is your name?" he asked abruptly.

Taddy's throat tightened. "T-T-Toady, sir." He was perilously close to tears anyway. Did the man intend reporting him to Mrs. Mainyard? Would he be asked to leave after so few days?

Almost as if in answer to his question, the man shrugged indifferently and said, "For your information, I don't expect to tell anyone about this. Please see, though, that nothing careless like this happens again."

Coat over his arm, Taddy knew he was being closely observed all the way to the hall rack. He felt as if his knees would give out under him as he reached up to hang the coat on the rack. What if he dropped that too? He made very certain the coat was firmly secured before he released his quivering hands.

"And now," the man said, "you may announce to your mistress that Mr. Graves . . . ah, here you are, my dear!"

For at that moment, Mrs. Mainyard rushed through the drawing room door, her skirts sweeping gracefully out from her slender ankles. In her afternoon dress of watered blue silk, with cascades of delicate lace setting off the diamond pendant that sparkled at her throat, she seemed more beautiful than ever.

Taddy, unfortunately, was caught standing by the coat-rack. He remembered Mrs. Fry's warning that servants should be as "invisible" as possible at all times. Even though the man, Mr. Graves, had ceased to pay any further attention to him, and Mrs. Mainyard's attention was totally directed at her visitor, Taddy wondered how "invisible" he would be if seen scurrying past them to the kitchen. He quickly decided instead to slip through the doorway to the dining room. Then, with his back pressed against the open door, he peeked into the hall. As soon as everyone had left, he would escape back to the kitchen.

"John!" exclaimed Mrs. Mainyard, stretching out her hand. "How wonderful to have you back! It has seemed a very long week. Did you conclude your business in New York successfully?"

Mr. Graves nodded, folding her hand between both of his own. He looked at her with a warm and telling smile. "And it has seemed a long week, indeed, to me as well, Elizabeth!"

Was this the same frightening man with the ugly temper, the man who had grabbed Taddy by the collar only moments earlier? It was impossible to believe!

Mrs. Mainyard needed a moment to collect herself after lowering her eyes and blushing prettily. "You know," she said, "I heard the bell while I was in the library and thought it might be you. Then when you weren't announced, I thought you had gone right back out again!"

Mr. Graves laughed aloud. "Never! Never! I was just handing my overcoat to your young doorman. He's new here, I believe. You know, Elizabeth, you must be careful about the people you hire. You have checked his background thoroughly, I presume. You know where he comes from?"

"Oh yes, he's quite safe," said Mrs. Mainyard earnestly. "He's the nephew of the proprietor of a quite respectable local inn."

"I see!" Mr. Graves was all smiles again. "Well then, shall we?" He put out his arm for Mrs. Mainyard to take.

But before she could put her arm through his, her dark-haired daughter, Madelina, came bursting down the stairs and flew over to where they stood. "Uncle John! Uncle John! Dora and I have had the influenza, but I had it much, much worse than she did." Madelina gave a proud toss of her head. "Did you bring me a present? Did you?"

"Madelina!" cried Mrs. Mainyard. "It is very rude to be asking such a question. Why, your Uncle John has only just set foot in the house." Despite her reprimand, however, Mrs. Mainyard smiled tenderly at her daughter.

"Well, I'm sorry to hear you were ill, Madelina, but very happy to see you fully recovered," said Mr. Graves. "And as it turns out, I do have a present for you."

"But not," interrupted Mrs. Mainyard, "until we are certain that Madelina has finished her lessons. Have you, dear? Is teacher still here?"

"Oh, I have finished, Mama," said Madelina soulfully. "And teacher is leaving now."

She had no sooner said this than a tall man stepped silently down the stairs, a man with a long, narrow face and thin, moist lips. A man Taddy had seen in the tavern of the Dog's Tail. It was Professor Greevey! Taddy threw a hand to his mouth to stifle a gasp.

He drew his head back quickly and stood glued to the door, holding his breath as Professor Greevey came to the hall rack to fetch his coat. When Taddy dared to peek out again, he saw Professor Greevey nod curtly to Mrs. Mainyard and her guest.

"Good evening to you both, madam . . . sir." He appeared to be wearing a dark scowl on his face as he left.

"Now! Now, Uncle John!" sang Madelina as soon as the door had closed. "May I have my gift now?"

"Why, yes," Mr. Graves replied. "It's right over there on the chair."

"Ooooh!" squealed Madelina. She skipped over to the chair and proceeded to rip the gold cord from the boxes. "Are they both for me?"

Mr. Graves smiled. "I'm afraid not, Madelina. One is for Dora."

"Which is mine then?" asked Madelina. "Is it nicer than hers?"

"I believe they're exactly the same," replied Mr. Graves, with a knowing look at Mrs. Mainyard.

Madelina's lower lip dropped. "Exactly?"

"I believe so," Mr. Graves said. "But why don't you open a box and see what it is?"

Frowning, Madelina snatched off a lid and pulled from the box a beautiful doll with a china head, long chestnut-brown hair, and brilliant blue glass eyes. It would have been difficult for anyone to continue being angry with such a doll in her hands. The doll did indeed bring a smile to Madelina's face.

"What do you say, Madelina?" prompted Mrs. Mainyard.

"Thank you, Uncle John," said Madelina. The smile on her face grew brighter as something came to her mind. "Well, at least it has hair almost like mine. And no matter what you say, my doll will be nicer than Dora's."

"And where is the other dear child, Elizabeth?" Mr. Graves asked. "Where *is* Dora?"

"Oh, she has to stay in her room after lessons, I'm afraid," replied Mrs. Mainyard. "I don't like to say it, but she will simply not stop tormenting Madelina."

"But she *will* get her doll, of course, won't she?" Mr. Graves asked.

"Oh yes, of course she will," replied Mrs. Mainyard. "In time. But shall we now go along into the drawing room? I'll ring for tea. And Madelina, you may bring your doll and join us for a while."

Once again, Mr. Graves extended his arm to Mrs. Mainyard. The two strolled into the drawing room, with Madelina chattering away beside them. The last thing Taddy heard as he ran into the kitchen was a peal of laughter from Mrs. Mainyard. It sounded as light and cheerful as Christmas bells.

Chapter XII

Tea Cakes under the Table

The ice wagon gave a perilous dip as it lurched into a gutter. Taddy tightened his fingers around the edge of the hard bench and drew up his shoulders against the icy wind. Somehow, after a day at the Mainyard house, he could never get used to being back on the ice wagon with Lucky, bumping and thumping their way back to the Dog's Tail.

"Still got to come and fetch him like I was a royal nursemaid!" Lucky grumbled. "And him not doing one lick o' work to make my life any sweeter. Not as he did much anyways. But help is help, even from the likes of a skinny runt like him. I ain't going to put up with this much longer. I tell you I ain't. I'll dump him in the river first!"

Fortunately, Lucky was carrying on this muttered conversation with himself, as was his usual case, so did not require any replies from the company present. Taddy, therefore, could tend to his own deep thoughts. Today, he had more than ever to think about.

There was, of course, the beautiful Mrs. Mainyard, to Taddy seeming more beautiful every time he saw her.

Now had been added to his thoughts the terrible Mr. John Graves. How could someone like that be a friend so close that he was called "Uncle John" by Mrs. Mainyard's daughter?

And there was Professor Greevey. Taddy shuddered, remembering the narrow face and the slippery smile he had seen in the yellow gleam of the oil lamp in the tavern.

And there was still Simon, the frightening old man who lived in the cellar. "Dum de dum dum." Every time Taddy went to the cellar, he had to listen to that tuneless song. Now, no matter how hard he tried, he could not keep it from running through his head.

But most of all, Taddy's thoughts were of someone he had still not seen, not that day, not all week—unless you considered the reflection of his own face in a cracked mirror—Jeremy, his twin!

The wagon lumbered off the cobblestones as they neared the Dog's Tail, and Taddy was finally able to relieve one hand of the duty of hanging onto the bench. He thrust his hand into his pocket and curled his fingers around a paper package, stuffed down there as far as it could be stuffed. It was to be presented to someone that night, someone who was certain to be an eager and attentive audience to all the new events of such grave importance that Taddy had to report about his day. And then, unaccountably, despite the thumping wagon, the grumbling Lucky, the bone-splintering cold, and the darkness of his thoughts, Taddy found that he was grinning.

Beetle, however, was not in a grinning mood when the boys crawled under the table later that night. He refused to light the candle and was ready to go to sleep at once.

"But Beetle," Taddy pleaded, "I have a lot to tell you about."

"See here, Toady, I'm wore out," said Beetle crossly. "Whilst you been lollyflapping about in a nice, warm house every day, doing not much of anyfing as I can tell, and being well fed wiv proper food into the bargain, wot do you suppose I do all day? Why, don't you suppose I just sit around wiv good old friendly Neezer, eating my head off whilst we hold nice little chats, and never a moment having to fetch and carry, or stand about on one foot freezing to deaf whilst Neezer goes into huddles wiv a number of his charming friends? Is that wot you supposes?"

"No," said Taddy meekly.

"Also, how much help you been perwiding me when supper's over in the tavern?" Beetle drew in a deep breath to reinforce himself. "I ask you, how much?"

"An hour?" suggested Taddy.

"Ha!" snorted Beetle. "Ten minutes, and no more!"

"Well, I come to help as soon as Lucky brings me home," said Taddy righteously.

"Brings you home! And ain't that just somefing else!" exploded Beetle. "Wot kind of arrangement is that, I ask you? Wot's wrong wiv walking? Unless they supposes you might run away. But I guess," he added with a sniff, "cornsidering wot Neezer's being paid for your serwices, you're much too waluable to be let loose now."

This statement probably being true, there was not much to be said about it. Silence followed, although there was no deep breathing to indicate that Beetle had dropped off to sleep.

"Beetle," Taddy finally ventured, "I . . . brought you something."

"Wot?"

"Why don't you light the candle and find out?" said Taddy.

And then there was finally the sound of a match being struck. A tiny, wavering flame struggled and at last succeeded in flaring up from the candle stub, lighting up Beetle's dirt-smudged face.

Taddy already had the package out of his pocket. He unwrapped it quickly and handed it to Beetle. "Here, these are for you."

"Where'd they come from?" asked Beetle suspiciously.

"Oh, they're left over from teatime," replied Taddy.

Beetle snorted. "Teatime! *You* have teatime? Wot kind of job is that, I ask you?"

"I didn't have it," Taddy explained hastily. "I wasn't even there. Mrs. Fry served tea to Mrs. Mainyard, and her guest, and Madelina. She's over her influenza now, Beetle."

Beetle produced an enormous yawn, clearly not too overcome by this last piece of information.

"Anyway," said Taddy, "on one plate that came back to the kitchen was one of every kind of tea cake, with a bite taken out of each. I guessed it was Madelina's plate from what Mrs. Fry said. She told me to throw it all out. But I didn't, Beetle. I saved them for you."

Beetle examined the contents of the unfolded package with a practiced eye. "Almost as good as new, Toady. Here, have one."

Taddy shook his head firmly. "No, they're just for you."

"Well, thank you! Here, hold this." Beetle handed Taddy the candle stub, then stuffed the remainder of a jam tart into his mouth. "And thanks, I suppose, to Miss Picky-Picky as well."

Taddy grimaced. "I'm glad she left the tea cakes, but I suspect she wouldn't have if she'd known what was to become of them. She . . . she isn't a very nice girl, Beetle. Her sister Dora was being punished and couldn't come to the tea party because Mrs. Mainyard thinks she was tormenting Madelina. I suspect it's the other way around. When I was there the first time, I saw her pull Dora's curls, but Dora was the one sent to her room. Do . . . do you think I should tell Mrs. Mainyard about it?"

"Cornsidering my experience wiv muvvers ain't much," said Beetle reflectively, "I can't be certain. But my guess is no muvver, or anyone else, would like to be getting adwice from the likes of you. So *my* adwice is to forget it, Toady. None of your business is how I look at it." Beetle paused to lick a crumb delicately off a finger. "Next?"

"Next what?" asked Taddy.

"You said you had lots to tell me," said Beetle. "I'm glad for the tea cakes, Toady, but is that all you had to tell about?"

"No," said Taddy, greatly disappointed that Beetle was not properly impressed with his news. "There's lots more."

Beetle yawned again. "Like what?"

"Like Mr. Graves, who came to visit Mrs. Mainyard," said Taddy. "I don't think she knows what a terrible man he is."

"And I suppose you do, and wish to adwise her of it?" Beetle gave an infuriating grin. "Well, wot did he do that was so terrible?"

Taddy then reported what had happened regarding Mr. Graves, threading it with as much suspense and horror as was possible.

"Took you by the collar, did he?" mused Beetle when Taddy had finished. "Sounds about like Neezer. Nuffing much to that. Next?"

"Well . . . well then," said Taddy, "you know that old man named Simon I told you about, the one who lives in the cellar? Well, I . . . I think he might be . . . *stealing* from Mrs. Mainyard." Taddy, in truth, thought no such thing, even though he felt that someone like Simon must be up to mischief of some kind. Anyway, this seemed a good way to get Beetle's attention.

"You saw him stealing wiv your own eyes?" inquired Beetle.

"N-n-no," said Taddy.

"Next?" said Beetle.

"Well then," said Taddy defiantly, "did you know that Professor Greevey is Madelina's and Dora's teacher?"

With this, Beetle's head snapped up. "Perfessor Greevey? The one wot stays here at the Dog's Tail?"

"The same," replied Taddy cheerfully, having finally captured Beetle's interest.

"How do you know?" he asked, frowning. "It's not somefing Lucky inwented for nobody knows why?"

"I saw him myself," said Taddy. "And Mrs. Mainyard *said* he was the teacher. Is something bad about that?"

Beetle shrugged. "Maybe somefing is. Maybe nuffing is." He helped himself to a macaroon and stared thoughtfully at the wall. "It's just that Perfessor Greevey comes, and Perfessor Greevey goes. But nuffing's ever led me to cornsider as how much love was lost betwixt him and Neezer. Now . . ." Beetle was lost in thought again.

"Now what?" asked Taddy impatiently.

"Well"—Beetle lowered his voice—"this morning down at the docks, whilst I was helping Neezer wiv collecting ice from the *Silver Queen,* he told me to go wait on the wagon. Then I looked over at him, and wot do you think? Why, there he was, heads togevver wiv Perfessor Greevey!"

"Oh!" gasped Taddy. "Do you think I should tell Mrs. Mainyard?"

"Don't be a raving ninny," said Beetle, rolling his eyes upward. "Like I said, maybe it's somefing. Maybe it's nuffing. Look, Perfessor Greevey is a perfessor. Wot he does is teach. For wot we know, maybe that's all there is to it. He and Neezer might just've been having a chat about the wevver. You don't go running to Mrs. Mainyard wiv everyfing wot comes along, Toady." Beetle stifled another yawn. "Next? Or are you finally finished?"

Taddy hesitated. This next subject was one he still was not certain about telling anyone. Even Beetle.

"Well?" said Beetle.

Taddy quickly made up his mind. "There . . . there *is* one more thing. Did . . . did you ever see a boy that worked in the kitchen when you were helping Lucky deliver ice?"

"I did," said Beetle. "Name of Jeremy. You're not going to report as how *he's* done somefing terrible too?"

Taddy shook his head. "I just wanted to know if . . . if you thought he looked anything like me?"

Beetle sleepily scratched his head. "Now you mention it, he does a little."

"He's my twin," said Taddy.

Beetle rolled over, his eyes popping. "Your *wot*?"

"My twin," repeated Taddy.

"How did you come up wiv that loony idea?" asked Beetle.

"It's not loony. It's true," said Taddy. "You *said* he looked like me."

"How come you never said anyfing about it?" said Beetle.

"I'm saying something now," replied Taddy. "Would . . . would you like to know more about it?"

Before Taddy could blink, Beetle was sitting bolt upright. "Tell me!"

And Taddy did.

"Wheeoo!" Beetle whistled when Taddy had finished his tale. "You ain't Taddy Buntz, like you always thought. You're Taddy Who-knows-whatever. You ain't from New York. You're more'n likely from around here. You ain't just you . . . you got a twin. And you might just be in mortalest danger. That's a lot of is's and ain'ts. Wot will you tell Jeremy when you see him?"

"I don't know," replied Taddy. "I suppose exactly what I've told you. I . . . I just wish there was somebody I could talk to about it."

"You're talking to me, ain't you?" said Beetle.

"I mean somebody who knows Jeremy," said Taddy.

"Remember what Uncle Buntz said, Beetle? I have to find my twin to know who I really am. So I should talk to someone who knows something about him."

Beetle shook his head. "Too bad there ain't anybody like that, Toady."

"Well, I've thought about it, and there is somebody." Taddy shifted uncomfortably. "It's . . . it's Mrs. Mainyard."

"Uh oh! There you go again! You really got a case on Mrs. Mainyard, if you'll pardon the obserwation." Beetle compressed his lips sternly. "Now see here, Toady, considering the danger mentioned by you, you had better say nuffing to anybody, present company excepted. You wait until Jeremy comes back, and you can talk it over wiv him. Meantime, whilst I'm out wiv Neezer, I'll be inwestigating. I'll find out somefing, I promise you. I'm good at it."

"What if Jeremy never comes back?" said Taddy.

"No point in crossing a bridge you ain't even come to yet," said Beetle. "Meantime, my adwice to you is to say nuffing."

"Nothing?"

Beetle took the candle from Taddy's hand, blew out the flame, and thumped down onto the floor. "Nuffing, Toady. *Nuffing!*"

Chapter XIII

Angry Words

Bong! Bong!

The entry hall of the Mainyard house resounded with the final tolling of the grandfather clock as it announced the hour of eleven o'clock in the morning. This time Taddy had no delicate teacups to worry about. If anything shook in his hands, there was no way to tell it, for he was on his way to the drawing room armed only with rags and a feather duster.

From somewhere upstairs came the sounds of the girls' voices. A short while earlier, the doorbell had rung, and Mrs. Fry had rushed to answer it herself. "You finish scraping that pan," she said to Taddy. "No doubt it's just the girls' teacher." So the sounds from upstairs must signal lessons in progress.

As Taddy walked softly into the drawing room, he could see that the double-glass, curtained French doors leading to the library were closed. That could only mean that Mrs. Mainyard was there, working at her desk.

The drawing room itself lay silent and still in the cold gray light coming through the tall windows, and there was no sound from the library. With his mind bent on not disturbing Mrs. Mainyard, Taddy went to work at once. He had never needed the warning from Mrs. Fry not to "go clattering about like a herd of elephants." Proud that he was making little more sound than a cat's paws, he lightly brushed his feather duster over the wood carving of a green velvet chair by the fireplace. But after no more than two or three sweeps of the duster, his hand froze in midair.

From behind the French doors had come the sound of a hushed, angry man's voice! An equally hushed, angry woman's voice replied—the voice of Mrs. Mainyard. Both voices were so low that Taddy could not tell what they were saying. It was certain, however, that the owners of the voices had been having an argument, and that there had been only a momentary lull when he had crept into the drawing room.

Who was the man with Mrs. Mainyard? Was it Mr. John Graves? Were his true colors coming out, and would she recognize him as the evil man he really was? The voice somehow did not quite sound like his, but it did sound oddly familiar. Much as Taddy wanted to discover the man's identity, however, he knew he could not wait to find it out. For how terrible it would be if Mrs. Mainyard were to find him there—*listening*! Taddy knew he had to leave the drawing room as quickly as possible.

But he had no more than made this decision when he heard the click of the French doors opening. There now *was* no time to escape. His heart pounding, he ducked down, crouching behind the chair he had just been dusting.

"I think you will have to make a decision . . . and

soon!" The man's voice was controlled and low—but furious.

Suddenly, Taddy recognized in it a curious whispering sound, a sound that when once heard was not easily forgotten. Pressing an eye against a hole in the carving of the chair, Taddy saw the man stride angrily from the room and then heard his footsteps rising up the stairs. It was indeed no other than—Professor Greevey!

What could cause such angry words between Mrs. Mainyard and Professor Greevey? Could it be because he had something unpleasant to report about Madelina's or Dora's studies? Whatever it was must have disturbed Mrs. Mainyard beyond all reason. For Professor Greevey had no sooner left than Taddy heard the French doors closing. And from behind them he heard the sound of bitter sobbing!

When Taddy next saw Mrs. Mainyard, however, it would have been impossible to tell that she could ever have had tears in her eyes that day. She was then dressed in a handsome black velveteen cape, lavishly trimmed in red braid, and a hat richly adorned with black ribbons, red feathers, and one tiny white dove perched jauntily on the crown, a circlet of diamonds twinkling from around its tiny neck. She was all smiles, her eyes glowing as she left the house on the arm of Mr. John Graves. Beside them tripped Madelina, herself dressed in a bright red velveteen cape, her hair pinned back with a satin bow that fluttered atop her head like an enormous red butterfly.

Taddy, who was holding back the door for them as they left, heard Mrs. Mainyard murmur, "Let us hope that the next time Dora can be with us. But when her teacher spends half an hour telling me that she has not been doing her lessons, well"—she paused to smile gently—"I can hardly reward her with an outing."

So that *was* what the angry words had been about! And how much Mrs. Mainyard must love her daughters that harsh words about one of them could cause her so much grief.

When Taddy closed the door behind the three of them, however, he could not help wishing that the angry words *had* been between Mr. John Graves and Mrs. Mainyard. Might they not have ended in Mr. Graves storming from the house forever?

For once again, Taddy had been pierced by those cold, steely, calculating eyes when he had opened the door to Mr. John Graves. It was evident that he still did not trust Taddy. And that, like a coiled snake, he was waiting for one wrong move so he could spring on Taddy again. Worse than that—report him to Mrs. Mainyard. But it was certain that Mr. John Graves would never be given that opportunity. Not if Taddy had anything to do with it!

Chapter XIV

A New Friend

When Taddy left the kitchen, carrying an empty laundry basket to the cellar, Mrs. Fry had been preparing herself a cup of tea and a small dish of leftover tea cakes. But when Taddy returned, his basket piled with linens earlier washed and ironed by Mrs. Fry, her teacup sat still unfilled on the table, the tea cakes untouched. Mrs. Fry's head now hung drooping over her apron. She was snoring gently, her snores harmonizing with the sound of the tea kettle bubbling on the stove.

She looked so peaceful, Taddy did not want to wake her. At any rate, although he had not yet been upstairs, he knew that the linens belonged in a cupboard in the hallway. And he felt almost certain it would please Mrs. Fry to have the linens all put away when she awoke. So Taddy tiptoed right past her.

Taddy had always supposed there were only bedrooms on the next floor up. The girls' voices had always sounded so far away, he thought their schoolroom and their playroom must be in the attic. When he found the linen cupboard, however, he saw in a room directly across from it a dollhouse, two doll cradles, and a large white rocking horse, all signs that this must be the playroom. In the center of the room was a white enameled table with four chairs placed neatly around it. And, at the moment, in one of the chairs, sat a girl with her head down on the table, golden curls tumbling over her arms. Beside the curls lay a doll dressed in tattered white lace.

Taddy hesitated. Should he finish his chore first, or simply leave and return later to help Mrs. Fry? But Dora, for that was who the golden-haired girl must be, appeared to be soundly asleep. Quietly, Taddy opened the doors to the linen closet and began putting away the sheets and pillow slips. It was then he heard the sound of a deep sigh, followed by someone sobbing softly. Cautiously, Taddy turned his head to look over his shoulder into the playroom.

And it was just then Dora raised her head and saw him. Her face broke into a radiant smile.

"Jeremy!"

Taddy's heart somersaulted. Jeremy! She had thought he was Jeremy! He spun around to face her.

Dora snatched up her doll and ran to the door. But at the door, she faltered. "Oh . . . oh . . . you're not Jeremy! Who . . . who are you?"

"I . . . I'm Toady."

Dora looked bewildered. "But you do look like Jeremy. And you are wearing his very same clothes. There's . . . there's even the same patch on the sleeve!"

And oh, how Taddy wanted to shout, "I look like Jeremy because I'm his twin!" But firmly implanted in his mind were the warnings from Neezer and Lucky to say nothing "what matters." And now, added to that, was Beetle's order to say "Nuffing, Toady. *Nuffing!*"

"Is Jeremy your friend?" Taddy asked.

Dora lowered her eyes. "He . . . he talks with me sometimes when no one's about." Then she added quickly, "He gave me a present once. Would you like to see it?"

Before Taddy could reply, she was already on her way to a chest of drawers under a window. Still cradling her doll, as if she could not bear to put it down, she opened a drawer and rummaged in it. Then she pulled out a small object hidden in a back corner. She ran with it back to Taddy.

"Look," she said. "It's a beautiful shell."

A shell! And about the size of the empty space on the shelf in the cellar! If Taddy had ever had any doubts that what was on the shelf belonged to Jeremy, he could have none now.

Dora handed the shell to him. "Put it to your ear. You can hear the sound of the sea, just as Jeremy said."

Taddy did as Dora asked. He had never been to the sea and could only take her word for the sound. But he was delighted with it. Then, as he was listening to the shell, his eyes fell on the doll in Dora's arms, and he drew in his breath sharply. For he recognized it as the doll that must have once matched the one given to Madelina by Mr. John Graves. This one, however, not only wore a tattered dress, but had hair cut into ragged shreds and a china face cracked from forehead to chin.

Dora saw him staring at her doll, but she only hugged it closer as tears welled up in her eyes. "I love my doll. I didn't tear her dress, or cut her hair, or hurt her face. I truly didn't."

"I didn't believe that you had," said Taddy, thinking at the same time that he knew full well who probably had done it.

"Well, Mama thinks I did," said Dora, choking back her tears. "She's very angry. She says she only hopes Uncle John, who gave me the doll, doesn't find out how dreadful I've been."

Knowing all about "Uncle John," Taddy could only hope too that he would not find out. "Well, I think she's beautiful, anyway," he said valiantly.

Dora's cheeks flushed with pleasure. "Toady," she said shyly, "will you be my friend too?"

The speechless, delighted Taddy could do no more than nod his head.

"When Jeremy comes back," said Dora, "we can all be friends. But . . . but what if he never does!"

"Oh, he'll be back," said Taddy. "I know he will."

"How do you know that?" asked Dora.

"Well . . . well . . ." Taddy searched in his mind for a good reason, for of course he had none at all. But at last he found one and wondered why he had never thought of it before. "Jeremy has all his playthings still here on the shelf in the cellar."

Dora's eyes widened with pleasure. "Oh, does he?" she breathed.

"Would you like to come and see?" asked Taddy.

"I . . . I can't leave the room," Dora said. "I'm being punished. All I did was get two sums wrong and make a pencil smudge on my paper, but Mama says teacher is very angry with me. Mrs. Fry would surely see us and tell Mama."

"Oh," said Taddy, "Mrs. Fry is in the kitchen, but she's snoring away!"

Dora threw a hand to her mouth, repressing a giggle.

"We can go and come right back," said Taddy boldly, although suddenly feeling much less bold than he sounded. He began to hope that Dora would not agree to this dangerous adventure.

"Well, if you think it's all right," Dora said, rewarding Taddy with a shy smile.

At this point, Taddy could hardly take back the invitation! Dora finally parted with her precious doll, setting it down on the play table as Taddy picked up his laundry basket. Then the two of them set off for the cellar.

When they reached the kitchen, Taddy peeked in and saw that Mrs. Fry was still snoring deeply while the kettle continued to bubble merrily on the stove. He set down his basket quietly and motioned to Dora. Then they tiptoed across the room to the cellar door. At the top of the stairs, Dora hesitated. But Taddy somehow managed to produce a reassuring smile, and she crept behind him down the steep, dark stairs to the gloomy corridor below.

"Oh, Toady!" she cried softly when they reached the shelf with the cracked mirror over it. "I believe these things all do belong to Jeremy."

"I think so too," said Taddy. "And see, this must be the place where he kept the shell he gave you."

Dora turned to him with shining eyes. "Yes, it must be!"

Then all at once, everything became too much for Taddy. He could hold back no longer and blurted out, "Would you like to know a secret?"

"Oh, yes!" exclaimed Dora.

"Jeremy and I are twins!" said Taddy.

Almost as soon as the words were out of his mouth, Taddy wished he could take them back. "Nuffing, Toady. *Nuffing!*" He could still hear Beetle's words in his head. Well, it was too late now!

Dora's eyes grew as round and wide as her doll's eyes. "Twins? But . . . but . . ."

"I can't explain about it now," said Taddy. "I will as soon as I can. Promise me you won't say anything to anyone about it. Please promise!"

"I promise," said Dora earnestly. "But just think of it . . . twins! I *thought* you looked alike!" She clapped her hands with pleasure.

But Taddy was by now becoming truly frightened. What they were doing was dangerous for them both.

"We'd better go now," he said anxiously. "Come on!"

Shuffle, thud. Shuffle, thud.

Before they could take another step, they heard him coming. Simon! Taddy looked at Dora with horror. How could he have forgotten that Simon, with his sharp ears that heard everything, lived in the cellar? And it was certain that Dora had forgotten it too. His head poking forward on its skinny neck, the old man stared at Taddy and Dora with his half-blind eyes that seemed to be hiding a sharp, searching gleam.

"Ho, ho! Little Dora and little Toady come to call on old Simon in the cellar. That's nice. It makes Simon happy. Oh, I see you're on your way out. Finished with what you came for, did you? I won't keep you. Dum de dum dum."

The old man stepped aside, singing as he did. "Simple Simon met a pieman going to the fair. One is gone now, maybe two, 'ware, beware beware. Dum de dum dum, dum, dum, dum."

Taddy snatched Dora's hand and pulled her to the stairs.

Mrs. Fry was still snoring when they arrived in the kitchen, but she began to stir restlessly as they tiptoed across the room. Dora was pale with fright as she scurried out the door.

Taddy turned to face Mrs. Fry, who now had her eyes fixed on him with the hazy look of someone just awakened from a sound sleep. "Put away the linens, just as you wanted them, Mrs. Fry," he said. He sounded as jaunty as Beetle, though his heart was pounding so hard he could barely breathe.

"Hmmmmph!" snorted Mrs. Fry. But then, softening, she added, "There's a good boy!"

Chapter XV
Caught!

"Toady, you are a raving ninny! You are a . . . a certified dummy! After all my adwice to say *nuffing*. Nuffing is nuffing, Toady. Which means you don't say anyfing to anybody. *Anybody! Nuffing to anybody!*" Beetle could hardly think of enough ways to let Taddy know how thoroughly disgusted he was. The candle stub in his hand wavered dangerously, spilling melted wax drops everywhere.

Taddy, of course, who had vowed to himself that he would not tell Beetle anything about what had happened, had blurted it all out almost the moment Beetle had lit the candle under the table at the Dog's Tail that night.

"Dora! Hmmmmph!" sniffed Beetle. "She's the littler one wiv all the yellow curls, ain't she? Wot did she do, smile sweetly at you like Mrs. Mainyard? Toady, you really are a ninny!"

Taddy already knew that. But he still thought he ought to defend himself. "What difference does it make if I told her? She already knows I look like Jeremy. When he comes back, then everyone will *see* it."

"And wot if he never comes back? Wot then?" said Beetle. "Seems to me it's wot *you* were saying."

"I've changed my mind," said Taddy righteously. "If he was never coming back, why would he leave all the things he played with in the cellar?"

"Like wot?" asked Beetle.

"Well, like a top, and a skip rope, and . . . and a bag of marbles," replied Taddy.

"Hmm," mused Beetle, who had probably never owned such an array of treasures in all of his life. "I expect as how he *would* want to come back for goods like that." Then after a moment, Beetle gave a resigned sigh. "All right then, wot did you tell her . . . everyfing about everyfing?"

"I just said Jeremy and I were twins," replied Taddy. "That's all, Beetle. Then I asked her not to tell anyone, and she promised."

Beetle shook his head, as if none of this could be believed. "Well, at least nobody else heard you telling about it."

This statement was met with deadly silence on Taddy's part.

"Nobody else *did* hear, did they, Toady?" Beetle repeated.

Silence.

"See here, Toady, did somebody else hear somefing, or didn't they?" Beetle was clearly not going to let this drop.

"Maybe . . . maybe Simon did," Taddy finally admitted in a fading voice.

Beetle exploded. "Simon! Ain't he the one you said steals things?"

"Maybe he doesn't," said Taddy.

"Maybe he doesn't!" Beetle slapped his forehead. "And likewise maybe he does, and who knows what else. Worse and worse! Well, there's nuffing to do now but wait. Maybe when this Jeremy comes back, there won't be anyfing to anyfing, and we'll bofe of us end up prize ninnies. You ready to serve tea cakes now?"

"They're getting dry," said Taddy, opening up a package smuggled care of his pocket into the Dog's Tail again. "At least Mrs. Fry says so. It's why she told me to throw them out."

"Ha!" said Beetle. "Your Mrs. Fry ought to have a go at wot we get to eat here. Why, these ain't even had a nibble taken out of them. You having one tonight?"

"I guess I will," replied Taddy, relieved at having got through his confession to Beetle and still finding himself alive.

Now there followed a contented silence as the two of them munched respectively on a lemon and a raspberry tart. Beetle was staring off somewhere over Taddy's shoulder and appeared to be deep in thought. "Toady," he said finally, "I've got somefing I've been cornsidering telling you about. Maybe it means somefing. Maybe it means nuffing. But I've corncluded it's somefing you ought to know about. Here, take this." He handed Taddy the candle stub and began to rummage about under some rags stuffed in his corner under the table.

He finally found what he was seeking, a ragged bit of

folded paper. He carefully opened it up and tipped its contents into his hand. Then he held out his hand to Toady. "Here, wot do you think of this?"

"I can't see anything," said Taddy.

"Look closer," said Beetle.

Taddy drew his face almost right down to Beetle's hand, and then he saw it—a tiny something sparkling there. "What is it?"

"If I don't miss my guess, Toady," said Beetle, "it's a diamond!"

"It's so small," said Taddy.

"It's what diamonds are, ninny," Beetle said. "This one's no smaller than most, but I expect it's worf piles and piles of money."

Taddy looked at him suspiciously. "Where did you get it?"

"I never stole it!" Beetle returned quickly. "I . . . I found it, Toady. I found it in a place you'd never guess in one million years. And it's where I found it made me cornsider you ought to know about it. Fact is . . ." Beetle dropped his voice and looked over his shoulder nervously.

And saw, at the same time as Taddy, an oil lantern wavering in the darkness and coming right toward the table! A few ghastly moments later, and the lantern was sending a searching yellow light under the table. Taddy quickly blew out the candle, but it was way too late to be thinking about that.

"Well, what've we got here?" It was Neezer's voice, thick from its owner having partaken too generously of certain liquid refreshments purveyed in the tavern of the

Dog's Tail. The voice was followed closely behind by Neezer's cruel face. "Looks to me like two little ragamuffins enjoying a cozy chat and a bit to eat. Wouldn't you say it looks like that, Lucky?"

Lucky's face appeared beside Neezer's. "Looks same as that to me too, Neezer." His voice gave every evidence of his having enjoyed the same cheering refreshments as his companion.

"Come on!" Neezer growled. "Help me get 'em out of here."

Rough hands, hard as steel, wrapped themselves around Taddy's ankles. Pieces of the tea cakes flew out as he was dragged out from under the table. A separate pair of hands dragged Beetle out along with Taddy.

"Getting to be little friends, eh? Behind my back, eh? Well, two boys allus means mischief. You two planning any mischief, boys?" Neezer grabbed the shoulders of each and shook them so hard it seemed he wanted to see their heads knocked off and rolling on the floor. And it was certain he had no interest in receiving any replies to his questions. "Where do you think you get off having picnics in the middle of the night? Where'd you steal the food from? You ain't satisfied in getting it honest, courtesy of my generosity in the tavern?"

"And ask them 'bout the candle, Neezer," Lucky broke in. "Ask 'bout *that*!"

Neezer gave both shoulders a bone-knocking shake. "What was you thinking? Anybody here care if the Dog's Tail got burned to a cinder and us along of it? Lucky, something's got to be done about this here situation. You got any good ideas on teaching lessons? Why, maybe even the boys can come up with something. Any ideas, boys?" Neezer leered into their faces. As it was clear, of course, that no answer was really expected, no answer was given. "Let me see, now." Neezer tapped his chin with a finger. "Oho, I have it! How about a little stay in the icehouse, eh? You agree that's a good place for lessons, Lucky?"

Lucky replied with a stupid grin.

"Well then, take 'em out!" Neezer snarled.

"Both of 'em?" inquired Lucky.

"Of course both of 'em, you dolt," snapped Neezer. "Oh now, wait here a minute. We don't want to do nothing to fix it so anything happens to the puny little goose what's laying all them nice little golden eggs for me working for the Widow Main'ard. You just take Beetle, Lucky. Time he had a stay in the icehouse, anyways. He ain't been out there in some time."

Lucky grabbed Beetle by the scruff of his neck and lurched across the kitchen, dragging him to the back door. Beetle turned to look at Taddy just as they started out. For all Beetle's brave talk about the icehouse, Taddy could see that his eyes were filled with terror.

But Taddy also saw something else. He saw Beetle put his hand in his pocket and quickly pull it out. The diamond! He must have dropped the diamond in his pocket. No matter how frightened he was, Beetle clearly never stopped *thinking*!

"As for you, you little runt, you get back where you come from. And you stay there!" Neezer shoved Taddy roughly back under the table. "And don't you try nothing. You were lucky tonight. Next time I might have a mind for you not to be so lucky."

Neezer picked up the lantern from the table and stumped out of the kitchen back to the tavern. A few minutes later, Lucky stumbled back into the dark kitchen, uttered several oaths as he thudded into the worktable, and finally found the door to the tavern. Then Taddy was left under his and Beetle's table, in the dark—alone.

Chapter XVI

Forgotten!

The minutes ticked by. Taddy lay on his back staring up into the darkness. He was determined that he would stay awake until Beetle was brought back. It did not seem a difficult thing to do, for with his stomach in a tight knot and his brain churning, he wondered if he could ever drop off to sleep again.

How long would those two in the tavern keep Beetle locked in the icehouse? How many minutes had already ticked by? And then Taddy remembered the question he had asked when he had first been introduced to the icehouse by Beetle: "What if they put you in there and forget all about you one day?" And then had come Beetle's cool reply. "There's always that now, ain't there?"

So Beetle knew as well as he did that it could possibly happen. No wonder there was fear in his eyes! Taddy shifted restlessly on his hard bed.

The minutes continued to tick by. How many now? Taddy might have dared to crawl out and look at the small kitchen clock, but it would have been too dark to see the hands. And he certainly did not dare to light a match.

Match! That was it! He began a frenzied search for Beetle's box of matches under his ragged blanket—and found them. No, the matches could not be lit, but they could have another useful purpose. Taddy began to count off the seconds. "One and two and three and . . ." When he reached sixty, he set a match down on the floor.

Taddy could have counted without the matches. But despite thinking that he would never fall asleep, his eyes had begun to droop dangerously. Setting out matches would help keep him awake. "One and two and three and . . ."

One match after another joined the first one on the floor. Taddy could not see them, but he could feel them. And when he finally stopped to make a count, there were sixty-one. Sixty-one minutes! And that had to be added to the minutes passed before Taddy had started to count. Could that have been a half hour? An hour? Longer?

The whole of the Dog's Tail was now a deadly quiet. Still, Neezer and Lucky always talked in low voices when they held their late-night conferences in the tavern. They could very well still be out there with their heads together. And they must have lost track of time. Surely they did not intend that Beetle should freeze to death. Did they? Should Taddy risk their anger and go out into their lair to remind them? Well, had Beetle not done as much for him?

Quietly, Taddy slid out from under the table. He tiptoed to the tavern door and slowly opened it. And found Neezer and Lucky with their heads on the table, wet mouths sagging open, snoring! The oil lantern, its flame barely flickering in the airless room, revealed the bottle and two empty glasses that had done their work so well. Both men were dead asleep!

Should Taddy try to wake them? He could readily imagine the fury of a Neezer and Lucky groggily opening their eyes to see *him* standing there. Perhaps he should just go out to the icehouse and try to kick down the door, with Beetle's help from the other side. With Beetle's help from the other side, after he had been out there freezing for who knew how long without even the benefit of his jacket? That was grim humor indeed! No, there was nothing for it but to wake up one of the men. But which? Well, if Lucky had been the one to lock Beetle up, should he not be the one to unlock him?

Taddy reached out a trembling hand and gave Lucky's sleeve a gentle tug. But the only recognition that Lucky gave of having been disturbed was to produce a loud, shuddering snore. Taddy reached out his hand again—and then he saw them. The keys dangling out of Lucky's pocket! The small hand already by Lucky's sleeve drifted downward and slowly—slowly—carefully—carefully lifted out the key ring.

After snatching up jackets from under the table in the kitchen, Taddy lost no time in hurtling out to the icehouse. "Beetle! Beetle!" he called out under his breath, meanwhile struggling with rapidly freezing fingers to try one key after the other in the lock.

There was no answering sound from inside the icehouse. No sound of Beetle's voice. No scraping or scratching sound of someone from the other side of the door. Nothing! Only deadly silence. Taddy's efforts grew frantic. Another key. And another. And at last, one turned in the lock! Taddy threw open the door and went in. And found Beetle crouched on the floor. Lifeless? Taddy shook him.

"Beetle! Beetle!" he cried.

Beetle finally made a small sound in his throat, so small Taddy could barely hear it. But it told him Beetle was alive! Quickly, Taddy dragged him from the icehouse. Then, somehow or other, he managed to stuff Beetle's limp arms into his jacket.

"Beetle! Beetle!" he kept right on saying.

And at last there was an answering voice. "It's all right, Toady," Beetle whispered hoarsely. "I ain't dead or anyfing like that."

"Well, I really didn't think you were," said Taddy. He put his arms around Beetle and finally managed to get him on his feet. Beetle's frozen legs took him two staggered steps forward, and then he sank back to the ground. Taddy pulled him up again and this time put one of Beetle's arms around his neck.

"Not too steady, I guess," said Beetle. "Come to think of it, where's Lucky? How come it was you came to get me?"

"He's dead asleep with Neezer in the tavern. I . . . I stole the keys from his pocket." Taddy tried to sound as if this were something he did at least once a day before breakfast.

"Stole the keys! You *are* a raving ninny, Toady," said Beetle, unable to keep the admiration from his voice. "But where we going *now*?"

"Back to bed," replied Taddy.

"Back to bed!" Beetle's wobbly legs came to a sudden stop. "Wot do you suppose is going to happen when Neezer and Lucky find me back under the table, and they had nuffing to do wiv putting me there?" Beetle moaned. "You might as well of left me to die in the icehouse, Toady."

"Then what should we do?" asked Taddy.

"You go put the keys in Lucky's pocket before he wakes up and puts *you* in the icehouse," Beetle said. "After which, *you* go to bed, and forget about me."

"Where will you go?" asked Taddy.

"I . . . I'll come up wiv somefing," said Beetle.

"No!" said Taddy firmly. "I'll go put the keys back, but I'm not going back to bed or anyplace else until you have a place to go, Beetle. You wait here, and don't move until I get back."

The way Beetle's legs were behaving, he could hardly have gone anywhere on his own anyway. Taddy saw that he was propped up against the storage shed and then raced back into the kitchen. When he arrived in the tavern, he found Neezer and Lucky still collapsed on the table, for all intents and purposes dead to the world. With the keys safely back in Lucky's pocket, Taddy raced back to Beetle.

"I've come up wiv somefing," he said as soon as Taddy appeared.

"Where?" asked Taddy, certain that Beetle was lying. "Where can you go?"

While Beetle was searching his brain for an answer, Taddy was thinking of something Neezer had said. "You try running away, and you'll find we got more arms and longer ones than you ever heard of to snatch you back." And this was probably true. For Neezer rubbed up against a great many people, from the dockside workers and sailors who partook of food and drink at the Dog's

Tail to the captains of the ships bringing in ice for his ice business, the shopkeepers and merchants and home owners who purchased the ice, all the way to the local undertakers, Murdstone and Murdstone, Inc. Oh yes, Neezer did have long arms indeed! Where could Beetle possibly go to get away from them?

And then suddenly it came to Taddy that perhaps the safest place to hide from Neezer and Beetle might be under their very noses. For would that not be the place they would least think to look? And it so happened that Taddy had just thought of that very place!

"Beetle," he said, "you don't have to think about it anymore. I know just the place for you to go."

"Where?" asked Beetle.

But before Taddy dared say anything, he looked warily over both shoulders. For if Neezer had long arms, was it not probable that his ears reached everywhere as well? Taddy saw and heard no one in the darkness, but he was still not willing to take any chances. He leaned over and whispered a name in Beetle's ear.

But Beetle shook his head. "Wot if I'm not wanted?"

"You have to try," Taddy replied. "You can't be any worse off than you are now."

Beetle thought about this for a moment. "I guess you're right, Toady. So I'll be off now. Good luck wiv Neezer and Lucky."

"Not without me, you're not going!" said Taddy. And before Beetle could take a step, his arm had been wrapped around Taddy's neck. "I'm taking you, and that's that."

"Wot happens if you don't get back before Neezer and Lucky wake up?" Beetle asked. "You'll get tossed in the icehouse, and who'll be around to save you, I ask you, Toady? Maybe you just better escape wiv me."

"No," said Taddy. "If I did, I might never find my twin, and then I'll never know who I really am. But you mustn't worry. Just remember about me being the puny little goose laying all the nice little golden eggs, Beetle!"

Beetle remembered and, for the first time, managed a weak grin.

Now, with nothing more to be said about it, they started out. In the small hours of the morning, the streets were dark and very nearly deserted. An occasional sailor, shoulders hunched against the sharp wind, made his silent way back to his ship. Once a door opened suddenly and two figures staggered out, their weaving footsteps giving evidence to what their owners had been about. But who of these would be concerned with two small ragamuffins, one leaning heavily on the other and barely able to walk, for there were ragamuffins such as these everywhere.

Still, Taddy had the ominous feeling they were being followed. More than once, he made Beetle stop while he looked quickly around. Was that a shadow slipping into a doorway as dark as a coal pit? Who was in that carriage, as dark as doom, rolling slowly past them? Was someone inside peering out at them, someone who might harm them? Who could know? Struggling and stumbling every step of the fearful way, the place Taddy had thought so close seemed hours and miles away. But at last they reached their destination.

Beetle, however, faltered at the doorstep. "Toady, that diamond I told you about is in my pocket."

"I know," said Taddy.

"Well, if nuffing happens to me, I'm going to split wiv

you . . . even. If anyfing does happen to me, I want you to have it." Beetle struggled to dip his free hand into his pocket. "Maybe you best take it now, Toady."

"No," Taddy said. "You keep it. Nothing's going to happen to you. Or . . . or me either! Come on!"

They made the final step up to the front door. Taddy reached up a hesitant hand and knocked. Gently at first. Then louder. Then he knocked again, more insistently. His heart was pounding, for who liked to be awakened at such an hour as this? Even the kindest people could not help but be angry. And then, at last, the door opened a crack. An eye peered out. As soon as it was noted that only two little boys were standing on the doorstep, the door opened wider.

Two people stood inside, a man and a woman. The man was holding a lighted candle in a candle holder. Both the man and the woman were wearing flannel night robes and great white nightcaps. Their eyes were as round as the buttons on their robes.

"Good . . . good evening, Mrs. Diggles," said Taddy, for indeed it *was* Mrs. Diggles and her husband. "We . . . we're sorry to bother you so late. I . . . I think you have met my friend, Beetle. "He's . . . he's done nothing wrong, but he's in terrible danger from Neezer and Lucky."

Mrs. Diggles looked knowingly at Mr. Diggles. "Well, I wouldn't wonder," she said. "Those two, hmmmmph! But what can we do for Beetle?"

"Would you hide him for now?" Taddy asked. "He won't be any trouble, will you, Beetle?"

"No, and I won't eat much," Beetle said. "Just scraps off the plates, same as I do at the Dog's Tail."

"Scraps off the plates! Well, I never!" exclaimed Mrs. Diggles.

"We certainly will be glad to take Beetle in," said Mr. Diggles wholeheartedly. "Why, with all of ours, an extra little lad will hardly be noticed."

"Oh, thank you!" breathed Taddy.

"Likewise," said Beetle, attempting a smile. Then suddenly, without any warning, he fell forward in a faint right against Mrs. Diggles's ample flannel robe.

"Why, you poor little mite!" she cried, and instantly wrapped her arms around him.

Chapter XVII

A Frightening Encounter

The kitchen door from the Dog's Tail tavern crashed open sometime between night and early morning. Heavy footsteps pounded across the floor.

"Fall asleep! You had to fall asleep, you thickheaded clod!" shouted Neezer, choking as he tried to keep his voice lowered.

"Not till after you did," bleated Lucky righteously.

"And that's supposed to make it all come 'round all right, you dolt?" Neezer raged. "If you'd seen I was asleep, all the more reason you should of kept your eyes open. Now who knows what we'll find out there!"

The voices and heavy footsteps crossed the kitchen and disappeared out the back door. Taddy lay under the table, awake, his heart lodged in his throat, waiting their return. No more than five minutes later they were back.

"Bolted! Bolted!" Neezer groaned. "Just walked out of there simple as you please . . . and bolted!"

"Well, at least he's not froze to death," Lucky whined. "And we don't get strung up for doing it."

"Strung up!" snorted Neezer. "It's all you ever think

of. If that little wharf rat got froze to death, we'd of just throwed him in the river, and who'd ever have knowed it? Or much less cared? Excepting me, of course, on account of losing a good worker. Not as how I'd be stoopid enough to go mentioning it. Question now is, how'd he get out, and where's he gone?"

The footsteps halted, and a whispered conference took place. The footsteps then thumped right toward the table, and stopped. Big hands were once again clamped around Taddy's ankles, dragging him out.

"All right, where is he?" snarled Neezer.

"Wh-wh-who?" stammered Taddy, rubbing his eyes as if he had been asleep.

Neezer thrust his bleary-eyed face right up to Taddy's. "Who'd you think, you little runt? Your friend, that's who!"

"Is . . . isn't he in the icehouse?" asked Taddy innocently.

"No, he *ain't* in the icehouse," Lucky replied. "Why'd you suppose Neezer was asking, for his health?" A sly look crossed his face. "Did *you* let yer friend out, Toady?"

"Now, how was he going to do that?" Neezer snapped. "Break the door down? You, who's been complaining that he ain't got any muscles worth the mention."

"Well then, maybe Beetle came in and told Toady where he was going. Now, that's possible, ain't it?" Lucky said. "Maybe his memory's froze up, Neezer. Maybe a trip to the icehouse would make it come unfroze in a hurry."

"Maybe," said Neezer, "but I ain't taking the chance of losing *this* one. Anyways, Beetle's not stoopid enough to come back in here just to report where he was going, once he made up his mind to take off. But we'll find him, never you fear. And when we do . . ." Neezer's eyes narrowed cruelly. "Meantime, Lucky, we'll look for someone what will take his place. Fortunate for us, strays ain't hard to come by."

"What 'bout Toady?" asked Lucky.

"Nothing 'bout Toady," said Neezer. "Just see he gets on that wagon this morning."

Lucky gave Taddy a baleful look.

"Wish I knowed how that Beetle got out," Neezer muttered as he headed for the tavern, with Lucky trailing behind him. Then suddenly, Neezer spun around, his eyes glaring with rage. "I know how," he ground out through clenched teeth. "You tomfool, you must of never locked the door!"

"I did too!" sniveled Lucky. "Toady must o' let him out after all."

"Toady? You think he broke the door down, you witless booby?" snapped Neezer. "No, it was you all along!"

They were still arguing when the door to the tavern closed. And nobody had even noticed that Beetle's jacket was now missing! Nonetheless, Taddy's heart was still stuck in his throat when he finally crawled back under the table.

That morning, Lucky sat hunched up on the ice wagon, glowering and muttering to himself all the way to the Mainyard house.

" 'Twasn't me. I don't know how he done it, but 'twasn't me. If I could just find him. I'll show Neezer!" Lucky's eyes darted from side to side, house to house, shop to shop, searching—searching.

As was always the case, Taddy might as well have been

a bale of rags sitting next to him for all the attention Lucky paid him. Still, when the wagon lumbered past Diggles's Bakery, Taddy kept his eyes glued firmly ahead. He never even blinked and only hoped Lucky could not hear his knees knocking.

All that day, as Taddy dusted, polished, and cleaned pots and pans, he wondered if he would ever see Beetle again. How he would miss Beetle's sharp little face peering at him over the dancing candle flame! And how was he to do without Beetle's "adwice"? Why, he would even miss Beetle's lectures!

And now, with Beetle missing, Taddy would be the only "stray" at the Dog's Tail. Neezer and Lucky, therefore, would have only one boy to pounce upon—Taddy. Furthermore, just before he had left the Dog's Tail with Lucky, he had caught Neezer looking at him with the all-too-familiar narrowed eyes. Had he begun thinking Taddy might not be so innocent with regard to Beetle's disappearance? If so, it must only be the thought of the golden eggs that was keeping him from putting Taddy in the icehouse for a course in memory refreshment. Oh, how grateful he was for those little golden eggs! He must be careful to make no mistakes at the Mainyard house, so gold, in whatever form, would keep falling into Neezer's greedy hands.

Despite Neezer's watchful eyes, however, Taddy determined that somehow he was going to see Beetle. But until that happened, he was all alone again. For Jeremy was still missing. And in addition, Taddy was still being given his clothes to wear. Were they now to be Taddy's forever? If so, did that mean the original wearer was never coming back?

Had something terrible happened to him? Could the same thing happen to Taddy? Could whoever it was who had harmed Jeremy be led right to the Mainyard house if they had been told all? The grim questions drummed on and on in Taddy's mind. And who was there left to answer them? No one!

Bong! Bong! Bong! Bong! Bong! Bong!
The grandfather clock, tolling the hour of six, was a mournful accompaniment to the icy wind that had started up again. Taddy could hear the wind moaning around the back of the house as he started down the cellar stairs. It was hardly what was needed to improve his leaden spirits or make more cheerful his trip to the dank, gloomy cellar, enlivened only by the sounds made by Simon creeping up and down the corridor. Today, Taddy had been told to sweep the furnace room as well as fetch his bucket of coal. Would Simon post himself at the doorway, watching him the whole time?

Shuffle, thud. Shuffle, thud. Dum de dum dum. Ever since Taddy had been to the cellar with Dora, he could never come down without having Simon arrive, peering at him with his half-blind eyes. Oh, how Taddy wished he could take back what he had told Dora! How much had the sharp-eared old man heard? Whom did he know who might be interested in having such information? Taddy could not help shivering when he reached the cellar, waiting for the familiar, dreaded sounds.

But there were none. The cellar was silent. Deadly silent. Taddy took three steps forward and waited. There was no answering shuffle, thud, shuffle thud. He took several more steps. There was still only silence. He took more steps and then gave a sharp gasp. For the door to the old man's room was wide open. And the room was empty! The silence, once merely eerie, suddenly turned ominous. Where was Simon hiding? *Why* was he hiding?

Taddy started to run. Not toward the stairs as he wanted to do, but toward the coal room. For if he returned to the kitchen empty-handed, he would only be sent back down again. He must fetch the bucket of coal first. Breathless with fear, he had almost reached the coal room when he heard the click of a door opening behind him. He started to turn, but it was too late. For a steel-hard arm had locked itself around his chest. Steel-hard fingers were slammed over his mouth. He was lifted into the room, and he heard the sound of a boot striking the door and closing it.

He was in one of the small storage rooms heavy with the smell of dust and mildew. On a large barrel in the corner, an oil lantern flickered, barely lighting up the room. With an arm still around his chest and a hand still over his mouth, Taddy felt the breath of a mouth pressed up against his ear.

"Now, what is going to happen is this. . . ." The man's voice was low, but hard. And it was one Taddy had heard before. But whose? Simon's? Was the old man really strong, not frail and old as he appeared? Whose? Whose voice was it?

The voice continued. "I am going to remove my hand from your mouth, and I will release you. You may then turn around, but you are not to make so much as one small sound. Is that clear?"

Very clear indeed! As best he could with the hand over his mouth, Taddy nodded.

The hand was removed. He was set down on the brick floor. He turned around. And stood there, frozen.

For he was looking into the face of—Mr. John Graves!

Chapter XVIII
An Unexpected Meeting

Mr. John Graves was dressed just as he had been the first time Taddy ever saw him—all in elegant black—excepting that now his gloves and ebony walking stick lay on the barrel next to the oil lantern. For a few moments, he pierced Taddy with a searching look, saying nothing.

"I'm sorry I had to frighten you like this," he said at last. His voice was quiet and steady. Then he paused another moment, as if he needed to collect his thoughts. "Now, I know that you have no reason whatsoever to trust me. But that is exactly what I am asking you to do, Taddy."

Taddy? How did Mr. John Graves know his real name? For there was no one in the Mainyard house who knew it, not even Dora!

"I can see by your face this will not be easy for you to do," Mr. Graves said. "But you must do it—you *must*! For your very life might depend on it. I promise you, this is all true. So I ask that you trust me—enough to do as I ask. Can you? *Will* you?"

Numb with shock and fear, Taddy looked silently up at Mr. John Graves. Who was he anyway? How did he know about the danger to Taddy? Most important, why was he warning Taddy about it? Could that mean he cared what happened to Taddy?

But how, so suddenly, could Taddy trust him? And yet, looking into the man's eyes, unwavering and somehow not quite so cold and hard, Taddy felt that he could. That he *must*!

Slowly, he nodded.

"Good!" said Mr. Graves. "And now I'm going to ask you to do what I tell you. The instructions are simple, and I want you to follow them exactly. And whatever happens, you must not be frightened. Just have trust in me, as you have agreed to do, and I promise that soon all will be made clear to you. *All!* Now, are you ready?"

"Y-y-yes," said Taddy.

"Good again!" said Mr. Graves. He strode over to the barrel and lifted a parcel lying on the floor beside it. "It seems I am always bringing packages, does it not?" He attempted a wan smile in Taddy's direction. Then he swiftly undid the wrappings and held up a woolen jacket. "Here," he said, "put this on. You are going to need it."

A warm jacket! That meant Taddy was to leave the safety of the Mainyard house. But where was he to go? *Where?* Could he change his mind? Was it too late?

"All right, then," said Mr. Graves, "this is what is to happen. You and I will leave the house together by the cellar stairs leading to the street. It is dark enough that no one should see us. Once there, I will remain behind, but I want you to run to the nearest corner as quickly as your legs will carry you. There you will find a carriage waiting. I want you to climb into it. The driver knows where to take you. When you reach your destination, he will instruct you as to what you are to do. You may be frightened, but I promise you, you will have nothing to fear. Just have trust in me. Now, shall we go?"

Go? As they climbed the stairs silently together, Taddy had begun to think that he should not only go, but keep on going, past the corner, past the carriage. On and on until the mysterious Mr. John Graves could never find him again.

But when they stepped out into the street, Mr. Graves whispered into his ear, "Don't be surprised at anyone you might find in the carriage. Now, off you go! I shall be seeing you soon."

Someone surprising in the carriage! Jeremy! It must be Jeremy! Taddy ran to the corner almost as fast as the wind at his back. When he reached the corner, he looked over his shoulder and saw Mr. John Graves, gloves and walking stick again in hand, climbing the front steps of the Mainyard house. But Taddy never stopped to question what Mr. Graves might be doing. He was far too intent on reaching the carriage. And when he did, he never even noticed that a hunched, caped figure with broad-brimmed hat pulled low over his face sat beside the driver. All Taddy could think of was getting inside the carriage. He threw open the door and scrambled in. And there on the seat sat a grinning—Beetle!

"B-B-Beetle!" stammered Taddy.

"The very same," said Beetle.

"Wh-what are you doing here?" asked Taddy.

"Here same as you, Toady," replied Beetle. "Courtesy of Mr. John Graves."

"But how . . . what . . . why?" Taddy had so many questions, he hardly knew which to ask first.

"Wot you wish to know," replied Beetle, "is how come I'm here, and wot am I doing coming along wiv you wherever we're going. Correct?"

"Something like that, Beetle," replied Taddy.

"Well, it's this way," began Beetle. "I was in the kitchen next to the bakery wiv all the little Diggleses, when a man wot announced himself as Mr. John Graves appeared in Diggles's Bakery. I heard him asking about two young boys wot had come calling there the night before. As you might cornsider, Mrs. Diggles told him she didn't know anyfing about any such, and Mr. Graves was no doubt inwestigating the wrong place. 'May I speak to you private, Mrs. Diggles?' said Mr. Graves. They must of gone into Mrs. Diggles's parlor, because it's where Mr. Graves was when Mrs. Diggles came later to fetch me. She said it was safe to talk to him and to tell him everyfing I know. Especially about you, Toady, because Mr. Graves told her you were in mortalest danger. So there we were all squozed up in the parlor, which ain't any bigger than a peanut shell, talking about everyfing."

"What everything did you talk about?" asked Taddy.

"Oh, Mr. Graves asked when it was Neezer and Lucky brought you to the Dog's Tail," replied Beetle. "He asked wot your name was, was it really Toady? On account of it was Mrs. Diggles wot told me to reweal everyfing, I told him your name was Taddy Used-to-be-Buntz."

"That's how he knew my proper name!" Taddy exclaimed.

"Must be," agreed Beetle. "Anyways, I likewise told how you found out you had a twin bruvver, which was more than likely Jeremy wot worked at Mrs. Mainyard's house, but come up missing. And Mr. Graves kept on saying, 'As I thought. As I thought.' It's wot he said mostly to everyfing I told him."

"What . . . what did he say about Jeremy?" asked Taddy. "Did he say where he was?"

"Nuffing," said Beetle. "I asked, but he never said anyfing but, 'All in good time, Beetle.' "

"Did you ask Mr. Graves how he found you?" Taddy asked.

Beetle slapped his forehead. "Forgot! Wot a raving ninny I am! But there's somefing else I have to tell you. It's about that diamond, Toady. I told Mrs. Diggles about it same as you. I said if nuffing happens to me, half's to go to you, and half's to go to her and Mr. Diggles. If somefing happens to me, and you get it all, as promised, I'd like it if you'd cornsider giving half to them."

"I will!" promised Taddy. "But where is it now?"

"Still in my pocket," replied Beetle. "Mrs. Diggles said she told Mr. Graves about it for a special reason, and then he adwised me to bring it wiv me. Might be needed, he said, togevver wiv me at wherever it is we're going. Whooooops!" Beetle grabbed hold of the leather seat. "Here we go, Toady!"

And indeed, the wheels of the carriage had begun to roll forward.

The wind had started to whip snowflakes against the windows of the cab, the flakes making small clicking sounds as they struck the glass. Clop! Clop! Clop! The sound of the horses' hooves and the sound of the snow beating against the windows were all that could be heard inside the cab. For the boys had fallen silent, clinging to their seats and trying to keep their faces away from the windows. For they were, after all, both now runaways— both in danger. And where were they going? Neither one could tell. Yet both were trusting in a man they barely knew, and in Mrs. Diggles to have been right in putting them in his hands.

The journey proved to be remarkably short. They had not gone down too many streets or turned too many corners before they came to a sudden stop. The driver instantly leaped down, his companion more clumsily following after. They took guard outside the cab, one to each door. Taddy then cautiously put his face to the window, motioning Beetle to look with him. And then the boys turned and looked at one another in wide-eyed horror. For they were drawn up just one carriage-length away from—the Dog's Tail!

Chapter XIX

Dinner at the Dog's Tail

How could anyone mistake the building? There it sat with its tipsy shutters, its blackened walls, and its forbidding door. And who could deny the sign dangling from rusty chains, the sign with the grinning white dog and the tarnished gold letters, DOG'S TAIL! They had indeed been brought back to the Dog's Tail! Tricked— Taddy and Beetle both! Beetle now known to have a valuable diamond in his pocket! And with guards now firmly planted on either side of the cab, how could they escape? *How?*

Clop! Clop! Clop! Clop! Suddenly there was the sound of more horses' hooves. Clop! Clop! Clop! Clop! And another carriage came to a stop directly in front of the door to the Dog's Tail. The driver leaped swiftly down and swung open the cab door.

At the same time, the doors to Taddy and Beetle's cab were likewise swung open. Taddy felt an iron grip close around his arm and pull him out. Directly behind him, Beetle suffered the same treatment. Escape? Why, they were as much prisoners as if they had been locked in the icehouse! Beetle's jailer brought him around to stand beside Taddy. But then it appeared that they were not to move until the occupants had left the carriage ahead of them. A moment passed. And another moment. Then an exquisitely trousered leg appeared out the door, followed by—Mr. John Graves! He turned at once to assist a lady in a sweeping skirt and luxurious cloak fastened at the throat with a love knot of shimmering diamonds. She was no other than—Mrs. Elizabeth Mainyard!

Mrs. Mainyard! What could she be doing here? What kind of danger was she being led into? She must be warned. But how?

"Mrs. Main—!" Taddy cried out desperately. But the word was cut short by a wiry hand clapped over his mouth. There the hand stayed.

As soon as Mrs. Mainyard had descended from the cab, Mr. Graves held out his arm to her. She took it, but her steps faltered.

"J-John, whatever . . . whatever are we doing at a place like this?"

"Why, my dear, we are coming here for dinner," replied Mr. Graves smoothly. "I have reserved a table for us."

"D-dinner? Here?" Mrs. Mainyard's voice was so faint that it could barely be heard.

"Why not?" said Mr. Graves. "You yourself told me the place was quite respectable. And while it does not look like much, I hear the food is excellent, particularly the roast fowl."

The Dog's Tail respectable? A table needing to be

reserved? Why, Taddy would have been exchanging grins with Beetle wide enough to split their faces if they had not been so terrified and the moment so grim. Mr. Graves evil after all! What was to become of the beautiful Mrs. Mainyard?

The party of two entered the ghastly building, and Beetle and Taddy were immediately yanked forward after them.

Shuffle, thud! Shuffle, thud! The footsteps beside Taddy's had a murderously familiar ring. Old Simon! *He* had been the caped figure on the seat with the driver, the one who now held Taddy prisoner. Old Simon, who had no doubt heard every word of Taddy's foolish revelation to Dora! What was *he* doing here? What had this old man, who lived like a mole in the cellar, to do with all of this? Taddy felt his legs ready to crumple under him as he and Beetle were led into the tavern, thick with the familiar smells of food, drink, and wet woolens.

The room was filled, every table but one taken up by the usual assortment of rough patrons, most of whom with faces that had seen more of the world than was needed by any man or woman. And in this room stood the elegant, superior Mr. John Graves, accompanied by the genteel, sumptuously attired Mrs. Elizabeth Mainyard. It was surely a party the likes of which had never before entered Neezer's door.

He now stood bowing to them, attempting a charming smile, which in the end more closely resembled the grin of a hyena. "Mrs. Main'ard," said he, his voice laced with the finest grade of oil available to him, "this is an honor. Indeed it is, ma'am. Won't you step this way?"

Mrs. Mainyard, her face frozen, clutched her skirts as closely to herself as possible and followed Neezer to the empty table, which sat at the back of the tavern. It had been set with what was clearly the pick of the Dog's Tail china, which is to say the same china as on every other table, but with fewer cracks and chipped edges. Behind the table stood poor little Mrs. Scrat, beaming at the honor of waiting on such distinguished guests.

As Mr. Graves seated Mrs. Mainyard at the table, Neezer finally caught sight of Beetle and Taddy with their keepers at the front door. His eyes popped and his face turned purple at the effort of choking back an outraged growl. He took a step forward but stopped when he felt the restraining hand of Mr. Graves on his arm.

"A moment, sir," said Mr. Graves. He stood motionless, only his eyes moving as he swiftly surveyed the room. "Ah, I see Professor Greevey is here. Splendid! And a good evening to you, sir!"

Professor Greevey was indeed there at his usual corner table. He nodded coldly to Mr. Graves and made a sudden motion to rise. Only to be blocked by a man moving closer to his chair.

"Well then," said Mr. Graves, "it appears that we are all here but one, who I feel certain will appear shortly. So, to your places, gentlemen!"

With that, every grown man in the tavern, excepting Professor Greevey, Mr. Graves himself, Neezer, and the two holding Taddy and Beetle, rose up and reached into their pockets. A moment later each man had pinned to his chest a bright brass policeman's badge! Two of the men quickly ran to the front door, two others to the stairs leading up, and two more to the door leading to the kitchen. Then all six stood, expressionless, with arms akimbo, guarding these possible escape routes.

"Please take me home, John!" cried Mrs. Mainyard.

Mr. Graves peeled off his black gloves with great deliberation and laid them on the table. "You will be leaving in good time, my dear," he said.

"I want to go *now!* At once!" Mrs. Mainyard's voice grew shrill with anger. "What is the meaning of this?"

"The meaning of *this,* as you put it, is that certain people here are under arrest," said Mr. Graves. "And among them, I am sorry to say, is you . . . Lizzy Greevey!"

Mrs. Mainyard put her hand to her throat. Her face had turned ashen. "What . . . what do you mean by such an insult?"

"If truth be an insult, then it must be an insult," returned Mr. Graves evenly. "But the truth is that you are indeed Lizzy Greevey, still wife of Professor Greevey."

Professor Greevey now displayed his yellow piano teeth in a ghastly smile. "Surely there must be a mistake, sir. How did you come up with such a ridiculous charge?"

"Very easily," replied Mr. Graves. "From the city records. There it shows that a Lizzy Snapes married Mr. Greevey. It then shows that Elizabeth Greevey, same birth date and place of birth, later married Mr. Mainyard. But there is no record of any divorce between Mr. and Mrs. Greevey."

The smile on Professor Greevey's face grew wider and ghastlier. "A minor oversight, surely. This is hardly a reason for arresting this lovely lady, or me either, if it should come to that."

"There are other reasons," said Mr. Graves. He paused to flick a bit of lint from his jacket. "There is, for example . . . the smuggling of stolen diamonds."

"Diamond smuggling?" inquired the former Mrs. Mainyard. Her eyes were blazing. "How . . . how dare you, Mr. Graves!"

"And how do you suggest that was accomplished?" asked Professor Greevey, his smile grown considerably thinner.

"In a most unusual and, I might say, clever way," replied Mr. Graves. "The diamonds were frozen in winter's ice, then smuggled in on the *Silver Queen,* courtesy of your accomplice, Captain Sly, who should be even now in the custody of the New York police. The diamonds, of course, were kept safely in the Mainyard icehouse until they were used to adorn you, my dear," said Mr. Graves, turning to the now Mrs. Greevey, "or sold to pay the cost of the operation. Young Beetle over there actually has a diamond."

"Stolen from me!" shouted Mrs. Greevey. "He must give it back!" She stopped, her face draining of color as she realized what she had said.

"Beetle never stole anything, Mrs. Greevey," said Mr. Graves. "He simply picked up a sliver of ice fallen on the floor of the Mainyard icehouse one day when he was delivering ice. Later, when the ice had melted, he discovered the diamond in his pocket. He actually was planning to give it away as a gift to . . . to friends."

"Well, the only one he'd better give it to is me!" snarled Neezer. "He works for me, don't he?"

"That matter will be attended to in a moment," said

Mr. Graves. "I have not yet finished with charges against Professor and Mrs. Greevey, because what they are also being arrested for is . . . attempted murder!"

"Murder!" Mrs. Greevey began to slide off her chair in a faint, though she was quickly returned to her seat by a nearby policeman. The smile on Professor Greevey's face had entirely vanished.

"Yes," said Mr. Graves, "thanks to the sharp ears of someone considered too old, crippled, and blind to be of much use but to live in the cellar and tend the furnace, someone who did not pose enough threat to be let go with other servants when Mr. Mainyard died, your grim secrets are known. For old Simon, now standing in this very room, was fortunate enough to be by an open window to the Mainyard garden when Professor and Mrs. Greevey were reviewing their dastardly plans, and he heard all. *All,* Professor and Mrs. Greevey!"

Old Simon! Simon with sharp ears not used for treachery after all, but for *uncovering* treachery! Old Simon, now standing beside Taddy in the tavern of the Dog's Tail!

"What Simon already knew," continued Mr. Graves, "was that Mrs. Greevey had come as the 'Widow' Greevey with her baby to be housekeeper to the newly widowed Mr. Mainyard and *his* two motherless babies. It is not difficult to imagine how the lonely and bereaved Mr. Mainyard ended up marrying the beautiful 'Widow' Greevey. The Greeveys' plan was, it seems, that Mr. Mainyard was to be done away with, and Mrs. Greevey, complete with the Mainyard fortune, would then conveniently remarry Professor Greevey.

"What Simon heard through the open window was Professor and Mrs. Greevey rejoicing in the untimely death of young Mr. Mainyard, thus saving them the difficulties of taking care of the unpleasant task themselves. They were then only faced with doing away with the male baby, who by Mainyard tradition was to inherit the largest portion of the family fortune. How they were to do this remained the question. Old Simon, however, had heard enough.

"In the dead of night, this old man, half blind and crippled though he was, crept into the nursery and took the baby. Somehow, he managed to hobble with it to a place outside the city, that place being the cottage where lived the baby's former nurse and her husband, once caretaker to the Mainyard house. The couple took the baby in and kept him hidden from the world, educating him as best they could to be the gentleman they hoped he would be some day. Then the couple tragically died, leaving the boy alone, and with no knowledge of his heritage."

Throughout the relating of these events by Mr. Graves, Professor and Mrs. Greevey sat silent and still as stone. "Where . . . where is that boy now?" she whispered hoarsely.

"Right here in this very room, my dear," said Mr. Graves. He looked across the room toward the front door. "It's all right, Simon, you may let him come to me!"

Taddy felt his arm released and a gentle shove to his back, propelling him toward Mr. Graves. Slowly, slowly he threaded his way around the tables and chairs. At last he reached Mr. Graves and lifted up his face. Mr. Graves looked deeply into his eyes. Then, putting a hand on each of Taddy's shoulders, turned him around to face both Professor and Mrs. Greevey.

"Allow me," he said, "to introduce you to Theodore Oxford Mainyard the fourth!"

Chapter XX

The Twin in the Tavern

Crash!

The platter in Neezer's hand plummeted to the floor. "Toady?" he croaked, his face taking on the appearance of a man whose collar has suddenly become too tight for him to breathe.

"How . . . how can you be certain?" asked Mrs. Greevey, clutching her throat.

"Because of this!" said Mr. Graves. And he pulled down Taddy's collar, just as he had on that terrible day in the hall of the Mainyard house. "Here you will see a birthmark somewhat in the shape of a half moon. His father wrote me of it when he was born."

"You?" said Mrs. Greevey. "And why should his father have been writing *you*?"

"I suppose he wrote to me, my dear, because I, curiously enough, happen to have a similar birthmark," replied Mr. Graves coolly. "And, of course, he might have written to me because my name is John Mainyard. I am Theodore Mainyard's younger brother, and this boy's *real* Uncle John." He squeezed Taddy's arm as he spoke.

"But . . . but John Mainyard is in Australia," said Mrs. Greevey faintly. "I . . . I just received a letter from him."

"Easily arranged. Letters were left there to be mailed by a friend at regular intervals," said the now Mr. John Mainyard. "In any event, I made my own fortune over there, sold all my ranches, and decided to return here. I have long been suspicious of Theodore's hasty marriage after the demise of his lovely wife. And even more suspicious when you wrote that their baby boy had crawled away from his nurse in the park and been drowned in the river. For the newspapers I ordered made no mention of this. My belief, of course, is that you never even notified the police of the baby's kidnapping for fear he might actually be found! Needless to say, I had myself introduced to you under a false name. I concluded it would be much easier to do my investigating that way. Wouldn't you agree with me, my dear?"

Mrs. Greevey suddenly let out a piercing shriek. "What's to become of my darling child? What's to become of Madelina?"

"Well," said Mr. Mainyard, "I have already made arrangements for dear Madelina, who was, I might add, born *Milly* Greevey. She will stay with relatives of yours until such time as you return. She is, in fact, being transported there even as we speak. And let us hope that these relatives, who had ten children at last count, will do a better job than you have with that overbearing, mean-spirited, spoiled offspring of yours!"

Mrs. Greevey threw him a look of pure, undistilled hatred.

"And now, I think all has been said that needs to be said at this time," said Mr. Mainyard. "Gentlemen, you may take them away!"

With this, Professor Greevey suddenly leaped up. There was no trace of any smile on his face now, only cold fury. "It's all your fault, Lizzie!" he shouted. "Oh, you were not named Diamond Liz for nothing . . . you and your insane love of the stones. And I was madman enough to think someone with your beautiful face could want *me*. But it was only the diamonds you ever wanted, and you knew my cleverness could get them for you. Unfortunately, you were right! I put it to good use with my inspired smuggling scheme, and then greasing the way for you to turn from Lizzie Greevey into the elegant Mrs. Elizabeth Mainyard. But even with all the wealth at your fingertips, you couldn't get enough of the diamonds, could you? So the smuggling went on. Then you grew to like being the grand Mrs. Mainyard so much, you didn't want to give that up either, did you? And I was besotted enough to let you put me off for ten years." Professor Greevey shook his fist at her. "Ten long years, Lizzie!"

He paused a moment to transfix her with wild, flaring eyes. "We could have sold out and left long ago, and no one the wiser. Now, you have made a big mistake for us both, madam. You see what's become of your plan to catch the rich and desirable Mr. John Graves and buy me off? I gave you a week to come to your senses, but it was already too late. You are a fool, Lizzie!"

"I never would have had you back! Never!" screamed Mrs. Greevey, her face distorted with blind rage. "Worm!"

"Jezebel!"

"Snake!"

"Officers," said Mr. John Mainyard, "please escort

these two out of here and let them fight it out at the police station!"

"Trollop!"

"Viper!"

Professor and Mrs. Greevey were still heard screaming at each other as they were led out and ushered into the police wagon.

For a few moments, the tavern seemed stunned into silence. But the silence was soon broken by Neezer. He rubbed his hands with satisfaction, giving every appearance of thinking the worst was over, that he had escaped the law again, and that he could go back to business as usual.

"Beetle!" he shouted across the room, as if Beetle had not nearly had his life snuffed out in the icehouse, and his return was a matter of course. "Look sharp now! Dinner has still to be served to Mr. Main'ard and . . . and"— Neezer was having no little difficulty in squeezing the next out—"the young Mr. Main'ard here." He gave Taddy a hideous grin.

"Oh now," said Mr. Mainyard, "not so quickly, Mr. Scrat. There are still a few things on the list that need to be settled."

Neezer's grin disappeared faster than that from any Cheshire cat. "Like what, Mr. Main'ard?" he asked, all innocence. "I ain't done any of them terrible things like Perfessor and Mrs. Greevey. Di'mond smuggling! Murder!" Neezer's face worked itself into the most curious expressions as he attempted to look shocked.

Mr. Mainyard sighed. "No, Mr. Scrat, but what would you say to child abduction and robbery?"

"Child ab-whatshun?" asked Neezer.

"Stealing, Mr. Scrat, stealing," said Mr. Mainyard wearily. "I believe the police officers here have something to talk about to you and your partner in those regards. And by the way, where could he be? He should be back from attempting to retrieve Taddy by now."

Almost on cue, into the tavern arrived Lucky. The first person he saw was Neezer. "He's gone, Neezer! Gone along of Beetle, and no doubt both in the same place. I was right all along. I was! I was!"

The next person Lucky saw was Taddy. "What's *he* doing here?" Lucky looked almost disappointed.

The next person he saw was Beetle. "Where'd you find *him*? What's going on here, Neezer?"

Neezer, meantime, practically lost his thumb jerking it around the room to try to draw Lucky's attention to the company present. "Keep your miserable mouth shut, Lucky. You'll get us into bigger trouble than we already got ourselves in."

Lucky froze dead in his tracks, finally persuaded by Neezer's thumb and his warning that all in the tavern was not well. Slack-jawed, he stared around the room at the police officers.

"That Perfessor Greevey blabbed on us!" he blurted, when at last keeping his "miserable mouth shut" proved to be more than he could manage. "I *said* as how he had suspicions, Neezer. You trying to get cozy with him didn't do you no good at all. And where's your motto now . . . them what pays stays? I *said* as how you should get rid o' him!"

"Well, you got your wish," snarled Neezer. "They carted him away too!"

"You might just take these two away as well, officers," said Mr. Mainyard. "I understand you've had your eyes on them a long time."

"That we have, sir!" said one of the men.

"Oh, now," said Neezer, "some of you have et in my establishment. Can't we talk all this over? Why, you know my wife here, Mrs. Scrat, and what a respectable woman she is. She'll stand up for me. I know she will."

There was a pause as all eyes turned to little Mrs. Scrat. She stared timidly at Neezer but then suddenly drew up all of her four feet eleven inches as far as they would go. "I certainly will not!" she said tartly.

"Now, Jenny," whined Neezer, "what do you mean you will not?"

"I mean I *won't.* That's what I mean!" said Mrs. Scrat.

"Well then, what do you think will happen if I get throwed in the lockup? What will happen to my Dog's Tail? What will happen to your means of livelihood? You ever think of them things?" snapped Neezer.

"Yes, I *have,*" snapped Mrs. Scrat right back. "And don't you 'my Dog's Tail' *me,* Ebenezer. It is not *your* Dog's Tail. It's *my* Dog's Tail and always has been, for it was *my* money bought it, and my cooking that keeps the customers coming back. I just always listened to you telling me I needed you to keep breathing. And what I'm telling you is I can keep breathing perfectly well all by myself. You take him and Lucky away, officers, and good riddance!"

Mrs. Scrat seemed to have had the final word.

"See what you've gone and done?" blubbered Lucky as the men were led away.

"Aw, stow it away!" Neezer growled. "All you never

wanted was to get strung up, and that's what you ain't never going to be. All we'll likely get for what we done is a few years."

"I don't want a few years," mewled Lucky.

"Well, you should of thought about that earlier!" snarled Neezer.

It was the last heard before the officer closed the door behind them.

The next silence in the tavern was broken by Mr. John Mainyard. "Well," he said, putting an arm around Taddy, "I know the hour is late, and we have all had a very wearying time, but I think we should go back to the house and see if Mrs. Fry can find something for us to eat and drink. Mrs. Scrat and Beetle, we'd be honored if you would both join us."

"I'd be delighted," said Mrs. Scrat.

"Ain't anyfing I'd like better," said Beetle, whose eyes had grown as wide as the Dog's Tail saucers ever since he entered the tavern and gave fair promise of staying that way forever.

"And," continued Mr. Mainyard, "as we have an empty cab at our disposal, I would like to suggest that Simon go by Diggles's Bakery. And if that good couple does not think it too late, bring them all over too."

"But . . . but, Mr. Mainyard," stammered Taddy, who amazingly enough was still on his feet, since his knees could hardly hold him any longer.

"Please, Taddy," said John Mainyard, "I am no longer Mr. Mainyard to you. I am your Uncle John!"

"Please then . . . Uncle John," said Taddy, "what about Jeremy? He . . . he's my twin. If we can find him, could . . . could he come too?"

"Oh, Taddy, haven't you heard anything that's been said here this evening? No, that's not a fair question. How can someone your age have taken in so much all at once?" John Mainyard said. "The truth, you dear, dear child, is that your twin is waiting for you at home now. And she is that darling little golden-curled girl named—Dora!"

Chapter XXI

A Cozy
Conversation

Dora, Taddy's twin? But how could that be? Quite simple, explained John Mainyard as they bowled home in the carriage. Taddy and Dora, born minutes apart and named Theodore and Theodora, could quite rightly be called twins. And Dora was not required to be a boy who looked like Taddy, any more than Taddy was required to be a girl who looked like Dora!

But what of Jeremy? Well, to begin with, it seems that he never would have returned, for his family had moved from the city. Taddy was simply the boy hired to replace him.

But how could Taddy have been so mistaken about Jeremy being his twin? Also easily explained, said John Mainyard. For Taddy had wanted so badly to find his twin, he was quite ready to accept the slight resemblance (noted at one quick glance), and *make* Jeremy that twin. Dora, who was confused at first by seeing Taddy in Jeremy's exact same clothes, was then ready to believe the same thing. As for Beetle, he decided that

Taddy and Jeremy really looked "nuffing alike, or close to nuffing, anyway," and wondered how he had ever thought so.

This much was talked about before they arrived at the Mainyard house to tell the wide-eyed Dora of the amazing events. It is to her credit that despite learning of a new brother who had already become a friend, tears rolled down her cheeks over the loss of a wicked stepmother and the spiteful Madelina. But the tears were soon quelled, and they went to the drawing room where they were awaited by the rest of the party.

It was a remarkably solemn gathering. Overwhelmed by recent events, and overawed by the magnificence of the Mainyard drawing room, the guests sat stiff and silent as so many figures in a wax museum. Despite all the best efforts of John Mainyard, not much sound was heard but the snapping of the log in the great marble fireplace and an occasional embarrassed cough, quickly subdued.

Mr. Diggles sat staring at the toes of his boots as if he had never seen them before. The five Diggles offspring clustered, round-eyed, about their mother's skirts, clearly having been warned that their very lives hung on good behavior. Mrs. Diggles's only conversational offerings were an occasional stern whisper to them to "remember what Mother said."

Mrs. Scrat, whose tiny feet barely touched the floor from the tall carved wood chair where she was perched, looked as though she had seen a specter and been left paralyzed by the sight. In a chair beside her sat Simon. He had no doubt never graced the Mainyard drawing room before. Now, persuaded with great effort by John

Mainyard to join the party, Simon gave every evidence of wishing never to grace the room again. Every so often, someone listening closely might detect a faint dum de dum dum issuing nervously from his throat.

Even Beetle, seldom at a loss for words, seemed to have lost every one he knew sitting cross-legged on the floor beside Theodore Oxford Mainyard the fourth. Theodore Oxford Mainyard the fourth, unfortunately, seemed to have nothing more on his mind than exchanging shy glances with the golden-curled girl sitting on the settee beside her Uncle John, cradling her battered doll. Beetle occupied himself with staring at the drawing room door to see when the promised "somefing to eat" would arrive.

Then, all at once, Mrs. Diggles turned to Mrs. Scrat. "I hear tell from Beetle, Mrs. Scrat, that you make the best muffins ever. Mr. Diggles and I always have our ears open when it comes to baked goods. You wouldn't be above sharing the receipt, would you?"

Well, indeed, Mrs. Scrat would not! And think of Beetle remembering her muffins with all that had happened to him! My, did you ever! And after that, the floodgates were opened to cheerfulness and good spirits. For suddenly Mr. Diggles developed a great interest in Australian ranches and wished to know all about them from John Mainyard. Even Simon had a question or two about the subject. As for the young Diggleses, why, seeing that their mother's attention was distracted, the four oldest left the baby sucking its thumb happily at her feet and ran off to play tag around the pianoforte.

Then Mrs. Fry, who had been exclaiming under her

breath such things as "Well, I never!" and "Wait until Mary hears!" and "I always said to myself he was a cut above other boys!" ever since she had been apprised of Taddy's new station in life, arrived bringing teapot, teacups and saucers, and the best Mainyard silver spoons, followed by a tray of hearty meat sandwiches (taking into account that two men and two lads present had not yet had their dinner, said Mrs. Fry), a platter of thinly sliced currant cake, and (with many apologies) a plate of tinned biscuits. Assured that nobody minded tinned biscuits, and that the ladies thought Mrs. Fry had done remarkably well considering the short notice, she then won further approval by whisking away the Diggles's baby and its brothers and sisters to the playroom.

Now all was cozy and warm and comfortable, with silver spoons tinkling against cups and saucers and burning embers crackling merrily in the fireplace. And it was time for John Mainyard to speak quietly of all that had transpired that night, to answer remaining questions, and to talk of future hopes and plans.

First he explained how, as Mr. John Graves, he had arranged to make the acquaintance of the then Mrs. Mainyard at the city's Christmas ball. But even though able to become a close family friend, he could find little to confirm his suspicions as to what had really happened to the baby Taddy.

Then one day he was present when "Mrs. Mainyard" gave Mrs. Fry instructions for someone named Simon, who, it seemed, was caretaker of the cellar. John Mainyard remembered a man of that name as having worked for his brother. By the simple means of knocking on the cellar door one night, he succeeded in meeting Simon and thus learned not only the true story of Taddy's disappearance, but that "Mrs. Mainyard" might not even be "Mrs. Mainyard" after all!

In keeping with his plan of not arousing any suspicions about himself, John Mainyard hired detectives to examine the city records and to lose no time in visiting the Buntz home outside the city. The records proved fruitful, but the Buntz home was found to be deserted! Frightened neighbors, when approached, reported that the Buntzes had recently died of a dread disease, leaving no living relations but a young boy. And he had disappeared!

Where to look for the boy? was the question. Had he been told by the Buntzes of his birthright? If so, might he not try to return to the Mainyard house? It was a slender thread of hope, but the only one John Mainyard had. Yet it seemed doomed to go nowhere, for there was no sign of Taddy to be found at the Mainyard house. Nor had he been found anyplace else at the time John Mainyard had to journey to New York.

Then when he returned, here was a boy opening the door to him at the Mainyard house, with features so like ones of those who had been near and dear to him, it was difficult not to claim them at once! It had broken his heart, John Mainyard said, to see Taddy's frightened face when he had to act so cruelly to discover the telltale birthmark. But discover it he must without raising an inkling of suspicion about himself, for there were still things to be known, things to be proved.

Simon had by now, of course, also seen Taddy, and even with his half-blind eyes somehow sensed Taddy's true identity, and tried to warn him with harmless-sounding rhymes. Then he heard Taddy telling Dora of being a twin. Only he had the wrong "twin" in mind! This told Simon, however, that Taddy could not know of his birthright. But it also told Simon that Taddy must indeed be the same child he had rescued as a baby.

Yet even with the knowledge of the birthmark, and all Simon's revelations, one more proof of Taddy's identity was still needed. That was to learn where he had been found by that "proprietor of a quite respectable inn," Ebenezer Scrat of the Dog's Tail.

Frighteningly, this individual, never known for having any lost love for Professor Greevey, had recently been seen with him in friendly conversation. Might Ebenezer Scrat decide to reveal where he had found Taddy? And if the place was as suspected, might Professor Greevey draw dangerous conclusions and then attempt to carry out the plan never completed so many years ago? It seemed a remote danger, but no risks could be taken. The investigation must not only be carried out in secret, but with all possible speed. Yet how was this to be safely done? That question was soon, and happily, answered.

For the detectives and plainclothes policemen commissioned by John Mainyard were now tracking Taddy's every move and watching him round the clock to make certain not a hair of his head was harmed. That was why two young boys, one leaning heavily on the other, were seen when they left the Dog's Tail in the dead of night.

Needless to say, this curious sight did not go unnoticed, and the two were followed to Diggles's Bakery.

"So that's how it was done!" Beetle burst out. "I never could figger anyfing out as to how you learned where I was."

"And you see, Beetle!" exclaimed Taddy. "We *were* being followed!"

John Mainyard smiled. "You were indeed! And then *you,* young man, were followed back again. You led my men a merry chase! But it was all worth the while, for I found Beetle and gained all the information I needed to have. And you all know the rest!"

They did indeed, even Mr. and Mrs. Diggles, who had, although with some difficulty, been able to piece it all together from Simon's halting report in the carriage. Now, the ugly past having been dismissed, it was time to talk of the bright future.

First, however, John Mainyard took time to whisper something in Dora's ear. And it was then he learned that she was not quite the sweet, docile child he had supposed. For to his proposal that he wished to replace the battered doll in her arms, Dora gave a delicious toss of her head and firmly stated that she loved the doll no matter what Madelina had done to it, for was it not a gift from her Uncle John? She would not have it replaced. She would *not*! And did her brother not agree with this? Her delighted brother, of course, did. The chastened John Mainyard then simply offered to have the doll's face properly repaired. He did mention, though, that perhaps a new dress and new wig might not be amiss, for did not ladies buy new dresses and change their hair styles? Dora most charmingly agreed to that.

It was then that John Mainyard announced to all that, although wealthy in his own right, he did not intend to establish his own home. He would instead have himself appointed guardian to Taddy and Dora, and come to live with them at the Mainyard house until they came of age. This idea was met with general approval.

And what was to become of Simon? Well, John Mainyard said that he intended buying a little house for the old man, where he could have his own nice garden and vegetable patch to tend, and there retire comfortably. Simon, upon hearing this, objected to it on all counts. He saw no reason why he should go anywhere and he wished to remain right where he was. He did not think it at all right that he should be *pushed out* just when the baby he had once rescued had come back to live at the Mainyard house!

Well then, if Dora and Taddy approved, which they did wholeheartedly, what would Simon think of the gazebo in the garden being turned into a small cottage where he could live and tend the garden *and* the furnace room? Simon was not certain about this, as the cellar had been his home for such a long time. So he scratched his head awhile, and then dum de dum dummed a while longer, and finally allowed that he might consider that small a change in his style of life.

Of course, he complained, if he were not to remain in the cellar, who would be there to watch over the "little men" sent down for coal and to provide them with things such as marbles, a skip rope, or a top when they had a few minutes off for playing? How much happiness that had brought him! he said. And what joy to give permission for a seashell to be given to precious Dora! But what despair that Taddy would never stay long enough in the cellar to play with all those boyhood treasures carefully laid out on the shelf under the cracked mirror!

So now it was known that those things had been provided by old Simon! Who would have thought it? Well, Taddy vowed, he would be playing with them now, right in front of Simon's own little house in the garden. Simon could be certain of that!

As to what the future foretold for Mr. and Mrs. Diggles, well, they were quite content with their bakery, and had no desire to go anywhere or do anything else. They did hope, however, that they would be called upon frequently by all present, and were assured that they would be.

Mrs. Scrat, when asked, said she had no intention of keeping that run-down, dismal tavern known as the Dog's Tail. She did not think it at all seemly that a lady should run such an establishment. If Ebenezer ever returned, he would find her gone! For she intended to sell the place and purchase a little house where she could run a small dining room, open to the public. And a good riddance to the Dog's Tail. Let somebody else have it!

Right after this pronouncement, Mrs. Fry reappeared carrying the Diggles's baby fast asleep in her arms. The four remaining Diggles offspring all stood at her side, yawning and rubbing their eyes. It seemed that it was now time to bring this joyful gathering to an end. Everyone stood up and prepared to leave the drawing room. One person, however, hung back. It was Beetle.

"Aren't you coming along, young man?" asked John Mainyard. "I'm having the carriage take everyone home."

Beetle looked from side to side. Then from up to down. Then from side to side again. "I ain't got a home to go to," he mumbled.

"Why you most certainly do," said Mrs. Scrat briskly. "You are coming home with me to the Dog's Tail. To a proper room, Beetle."

"I thought Beetle was coming to live with *us*," said Mrs. Diggles. "Why we like him so much, we want him to become one of our own!"

"But I thought he was to come live with *us*, Uncle . . . Uncle John!" said Taddy, faltering on the name because it was still a name to be got used to. "We have lots and lots of rooms. Beetle can have one of them, can't he?"

John Mainyard put an arm around Beetle's skinny shoulders, laughing aloud. "It seems you're quite right, Beetle. You don't have *a* home to go to. It appears that you have *three*! The only problem you have in your life right now is to choose which one."

A totally disbelieving look on Beetle's face was almost instantly replaced with a grin so broad it seemed to reach his ears and right around the back of his head. And, as it turned out, it took him no time at all to make up his mind.

"Well," he said, "cornsidering as how Mr. and Mrs. Diggles got so many of their own, and don't need anovver mouf to feed . . . and cornsidering as how Mr. Mainyard don't need adwice on how to manage anyfing, and likewise don't need anovver body to look after . . . why I believe as how I choose to live wiv Mrs. Scrat. She'll be needing my adwice, and a man about the place for the heavy work. Besides she . . . she ain't got any boy or girl of her own, nor anyone else as far as I can see."

Little Mrs. Scrat beamed, tears welling in her eyes.

"Oh, and one thing more," Beetle said. "Mr. Mainyard, is there anyone I got to give the diamond back to?"

John Mainyard smiled and shook his head. "I have no idea how we could ever find the owner. I guess you'll have to keep it, Beetle."

"Not wot I wanted," said Beetle. "I just wanted to ask if everyone I promised it to would cornsider sharing wiv Mrs. Scrat, who's been good to me."

"I'm afraid that if your generous heart causes that little diamond to be divided any further, it will end up nothing but diamond dust!" said John Mainyard, smiling. "I wonder if everyone here might not agree to your keeping it yourself, Beetle."

All there nodded their heads eagerly to this suggestion.

"Well, then," said John Mainyard, "I shall see that you get a handsome price for it, and perhaps Mrs. Scrat can put it away for your education."

"My *wot*!" exclaimed Beetle. "Nuffing like that, if nobody minds. I'll run away first!"

"You'll do no such thing, Beetle!" retorted Mrs. Scrat. "How do you expect to come visit Theodore if you don't give some promise of becoming a gentleman? Anyway, we will talk about it later. Come along now. The carriage is waiting!"

Beetle meekly followed her through the door. But just before it closed, he poked his grinning face back in and said, "Don't this beat anyfing you ever heard of, Toady?"

To which there was nothing left for Taddy to do but nod—and produce a wide, happy grin of his own!

About the Author

Barbara Brooks Wallace writes, "I was never a mystery buff. I don't even remember being interested in puzzles and mysteries as a child growing up in China. My fondest memories of books were the Oz books that appeared under the Christmas tree with beautiful regularity each year (sent from America by Grandmother) and the Tiger Tim Annuals (which came from England via the local British department store). So it is now a mystery to me that I was ever actually able to write one." *Peppermints in the Parlor*, Ms. Wallace's first book for Atheneum, is the mysterious mystery she speaks about.

The Wallaces, Barbara and Jim, live in Alexandria, Virginia.